Kendall's scream pierced the still night and turned the blood in Coop's veins to ice.

Coop had already been making his way back down the drive when he'd heard Kendall's truck coming back to the house. Now his boots grappled for purchase against the soggy leaves on the walkway as he ran toward Kendall.

"What is it? What's wrong?" By the time he reached her, he was panting as if he'd just run a marathon.

She'd stumbled back from the truck and stood staring at the tailgate with wide, glassy eyes. Raising her arm, she pointed to the truck with her cell phone. She worked her jaw but couldn't form any words—no coherent words, anyway.

He pried the phone from her stiff fingers, aimed the light at the truck bed and jumped onto the bumper. The phone illuminated a light-colored tarp with something rolled up in it.

"I-it's a body."

SINGLE FATHER SHERIFF

Carol Ericson

———

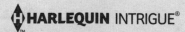

To my sister Janice, my cheerleader

Recycling programs
for this product may
not exist in your area.

ISBN-13: 978-0-373-69923-0

Single Father Sheriff

Copyright © 2016 by Carol Ericson

This edition published by arrangement with Harlequin Books S.A.

For questions and comments about the quality of this book, please contact us at CustomerService@Harlequin.com.

® and TM are trademarks of Harlequin Enterprises Limited or its corporate affiliates. Trademarks indicated with ® are registered in the United States Patent and Trademark Office, the Canadian Intellectual Property Office and in other countries.

Printed in U.S.A.

™ www.Harlequin.com

Carol Ericson is a bestselling, award-winning author of more than forty books. She has an eerie fascination for true-crime stories, a love of film noir and a weakness for reality TV, all of which fuel her imagination to create her own tales of murder, mayhem and mystery. To find out more about Carol and her current projects, please visit her website at www.carolericson.com, "where romance flirts with danger."

Books by Carol Ericson

Harlequin Intrigue

Target: Timberline

Single Father Sheriff

Brothers in Arms: Retribution

Under Fire
The Pregnancy Plot
Navy SEAL Spy
Secret Agent Santa

Brody Law

The Bridge
The District
The Wharf
The Hill

Visit the Author Profile page at Harlequin.com for more titles.

CAST OF CHARACTERS

Kendall Rush—Her traumatic past comes back to haunt her when she returns to Timberline, Washington. She wants nothing to do with the current kidnappings... until she meets the sexy sheriff who needs her help.

Cooper Sloane—The sheriff of Timberline and a single dad, he's counting on Kendall to give him some information that will help him find two missing children.

Kayla Rush—Kendall's twin was kidnapped twenty-five years ago and Kendall has never gotten over it.

Stevie Carson—One of the original Timberline Trio, whose brother, Wyatt, is still suffering from the trauma.

Steffi Sloane—Coop's daughter lost her mother, but she's not so sure she wants a replacement.

Chuck Rawlings—This registered sex offender was investigated during the first set of kidnappings, and he might just be involved in the second set.

Gary Binder—A recovering drug addict and ex-con, he's trying to get his life back on track.

Wyatt Carson—Like Kendall, he has had to deal with the trauma of losing a sibling to a kidnapper, but the tragedy has brought him to a very dark place.

Dr. Jules Shipman—Coop blames this therapist for his wife's suicide.

Agent Matt Waterford—The FBI agent assigned to the kidnapping task force whose inability to think outside the box may end up getting three children killed.

Annie Foster—A member of the Quileute tribe, she warns Kendall that the local members of the tribe fear there is an even more sinister purpose to the kidnappings than ransom or trafficking.

Chapter One

"Let go of my sister." The little girl with the dark pigtails scrunched up her face and stomped on the masked stranger's foot.

He reached out one hand and squeezed her shoulder, but she twisted out of his grasp and renewed her assault on him, pummeling his thigh with her tiny fists.

The monster growled and swatted at the little girl, knocking her to the floor. "You're too much damned trouble."

As he backed up toward the door, carrying her sleeping twin over one shoulder, the girl lunged at his legs. "Put her down!"

With his free hand, the stranger clamped down on the top of her head, digging his fingers into her scalp, holding her at bay. As he gave one last push, he yanked off the pink ribbon tied around one of her pigtails and left her sprawled on the floor.

She scrambled to her knees, rubbing the back of her head. Whatever happened, she couldn't let the man take Kayla out that door. She crawled toward his legs once more.

"Your parents are gonna wish I took you instead of this one." Then he kicked her in the face and everything went black.

KENDALL RAN A HAND across her jaw as she dropped to her knees in front of the door. "I'm sorry, Kayla. I'm sorry I couldn't save you."

Common sense and her therapist's assertion that a five-year-old couldn't have done much against a full-grown man intent on kidnapping her twin were no match for twenty-five years of guilt.

Kendall leaned forward, touching her forehead to the hardwood floor. She'd relegated the trauma of that event to her past, stuffed it down, shoved it into the dark corner where it belonged. Now someone in Timberline was bringing it all back and that sheriff expected her to help in the investigation of a new set of kidnappings.

If she could help, she would've done something twenty-five years ago to bring her sister home. Her heart broke for the two families torn apart by the same torment that destroyed her own family but she couldn't save them, and that sheriff would have to look elsewhere for help solving the crimes.

She'd come back to Timberline to sell her aunt's house—nothing more, nothing less. It just so happened that her aunt's house was the same house where she'd spent many days as a child, the same house from which someone abducted her twin sister and had knocked her out cold.

Raising her head, she zeroed in on the front door. She could picture it all again—the stranger with the ski mask, her sleeping sister thrown over one of his shoulders. Much of what followed had been a blur of hysterical parents, soft-spoken police officers, sleepless nights and bad dreams.

She still had the bad dreams.

Someone knocked on the door, and her muscles tensed as she wedged her fingers against the wood floor like a runner ready to shoot out of the blocks.

"Who's there?"

"It's Wyatt, Wyatt Carson."

Her thundering heartbeat slowed only a fraction when she heard Wyatt's voice. If she was looking for someone to bring her out of the throes of these unpleasant memories, it wasn't Wyatt.

Clearing her throat, she lumbered to her feet. "Hold on, Wyatt."

She brushed the dust from her knees and pushed the hair back from her face. Squaring her shoulders, she pasted on a smile. Then she swung open the door to greet the last man she wanted to see right now.

"Hey, Wyatt. How'd you know I was back?"

"Kendall." He swooped in for a hug, engulfing her in flannel and the tingly scent of pine. "You know Timberline. Word travels fast."

"Supersonic." She mumbled her words into his shoulder since he still held her fast. She stiffened, arching her back, and he got the hint.

When he released her, she shoved her hands in her pockets and smiled up at him. "I just arrived yesterday and took one trip to the grocery store."

He snapped his fingers. "That must've been it. I

heard you were back when I was getting coffee at Common Grounds this morning."

"Come on in." She stepped back from the door. "How have you been? Still the town's best plumber?"

"One of the town's only plumbers." He puffed up his chest anyway.

"Do you want something to drink?" She held her breath, hoping he'd say no.

"Sure, a can of pop if you have it."

"I do." She moved past him to go into the kitchen. She ducked into the refrigerator and grabbed a can of soda. "Do you want a glass?"

She cocked her head, waiting for an answer from the other room. "Wyatt?"

"Yeah?"

She jumped, the wet can slipping from her hand and bouncing on the linoleum floor. Wyatt moved silently for a big man.

"Sorry." He pushed off of the doorjamb and crowded into the small kitchen space.

Before she could recover her breath, he crouched down and snagged the can. "Do you have another? I don't want to spray the kitchen with pop."

She tugged on the fridge door and swept another can from the shelf.

He exchanged cans with her. "You're jumpy. Is it this house?"

Her gaze met his dark brown eyes, luminous in the pasty pallor of his face—a sure sign of a Timberline native.

Ducking back into the fridge, she shoved the dented can toward the back of the shelf.

"You just startled me, Wyatt. I'm not reliving any memories." She waved her arm around the kitchen to deflect attention from her lie. "This is just a house, not a living, breathing entity."

"I'm surprised you'd have that outlook, Kendall." He snapped the tab on his can of soda and slurped the fizzy liquid from the rim. "I mean, since you're a psychiatrist."

"I'm a psychologist, not a psychiatrist."

"Whatever. Don't you dig into people's memories? Pick their brains? Find out what makes them tick?"

"It doesn't work that way, Wyatt. You get out of therapy what you put into it. My clients pick their own brains. I'm just there to facilitate."

"Wish plumbing worked that way." He slapped the thigh of his denims and took another gulp of his soda. "Seriously, if you ever want to talk about what happened twenty-five years ago, I'm your man."

"I think we've talked it all out by now, don't you?"

"But you and me—" he wagged his finger back and forth between them "—never really talked about it—not when we were kids right after it happened and not as adults."

Folding her arms, she leaned against the kitchen counter. "Do you need to talk about it? Have you ever seen a therapist?"

He held up his hands, his callous palms facing her. "I'm not asking for a freebie or anything, Kendall."

A warm flush invaded her cheeks, and she swiped a damp sponge across the countertop. "I didn't think you were, but if you're interested in seeing someone

I can do a little research and find a good therapist in the area for you."

"Nah, I'm good. I just thought…" He shrugged his shoulders. "You know, you and me, since we both went through the same thing. You lost your sister and I lost my brother to the same kidnapper. We just never really discussed our feelings with each other."

Years ago she'd vomited up these feelings to her own therapist until she'd emptied her gut, and she had no intention of dredging them up again with Wyatt Carson…or with anyone.

"It happened. I was sad, and we all moved on." She brushed her fingertips along the soft flannel of his shirtsleeve. "If you need—if you want more closure, my offer stands. I can vet some therapists in the area for you."

He downed the rest of his drink and crushed the can in his hand. "Don't tell me you don't know what's going on, Kendall."

"I know." She took a deep breath. "Two children have been kidnapped."

"I moved on, too." He toyed with the tab on his can until he twisted it off. "I had it all packed away—until this. I just figured that's why you came back."

"N-no. Aunt Cass left this house to me when she passed, and I'm here to settle her things and sell the property."

"Aunt Cass passed away ten months ago."

"You know, probate, legal stuff." She flicked her fingers in the air. "All that had to get sorted out, and I had a few work obligations to handle first."

"If you say so." He held up the mangled can. "Trash?"

"Recycle bin in here." She tapped the cupboard under the sink with her toe.

He tossed the can into the plastic bin and shoved his hands into his pockets. "You know, you might not be able to slip in and out of Timberline so easy."

"What does that mean?"

"There's a new sheriff in town—literally, or at least new to you. He's actually been here about five years." Wyatt tapped the side of his head. "He's een picking my brain, and I'm pretty sure he's gonna w ant to pick yours, too, once he knows you're back."

Her heart flip-flopped. "I'd heard that from some-one else—that he wanted to talk to me."

"Timberline's still a small town, even with I ver-green Software going in. Coop must've heard you w re back already."

"Coop?"

"Sheriff Cooper Sloane. He moved here about five years ago."

"Yeah, you said that. Isn't the FBI involved?"

"As far as I heard they were. I think they set up op-erations just outside of Timberline. There are a couple of agents out here poking around, setting up taps on the families' phones, waiting for ransom instructions."

Kendall pressed her spine against the counter, try-ing to stop the shiver snaking up her back. There had been no ransom demands twenty-five years ago for the Timberline Trio—the three children who'd been kid-napped. Would there be any now?

"Anything?"

"Not yet and it's already been almost three weeks." Wyatt scratched his chin. "That's one of the reasons Coop's so interested in talking to all the players from the past. He sees some similarities in the cases, but the FBI agents aren't all that interested in what happened twenty-five years ago."

"Well, I'm not going to be much help." She pushed off the counter. "But I do need to get back to work if I hope to get this place on the market."

"Don't worry. I'm outta here." Wyatt exited the small kitchen and stood in the middle of the living room with his hands on his hips, surveying the room as if he could see the ghosts that still lingered. "If you ever want to talk, you know where to find me."

"I appreciate that, Wyatt." She took two steps into the room and gave the big man a hug, assuaging the pangs of guilt she had over her uncharitable thoughts about him. Had he sensed her reluctance to talk to him? She squeezed harder.

"Take care, Wyatt. Maybe we'll catch up a little more over lunch while I'm here."

"I'd like that." He broke their clinch. "Now I'd better head over to the police station."

As much practice as she'd had schooling her face into a bland facade for her clients, she must've revealed her uneasiness to Wyatt.

His dark eyebrows jumped to his hairline. "This is just a plumbing job, not an interrogation."

"Honestly, Wyatt, what you plan to do is your business." She smoothed her hands over her face. "I'd rather leave it in the past."

"I hear ya." He saluted. "Let's have that lunch real soon."

She closed the door behind him and touched her forehead to the doorjamb. Wyatt didn't even have to be an amateur psychologist to figure out she was protesting way too much.

She'd need a supersize session with her own therapist once she left this rain-soaked place and returned to Phoenix.

Taking a deep breath, she brushed her hands together and grabbed an empty box. She stationed herself in front of the cabinet shelf that sported a stack of newspapers.

She dusted each item in her aunt's collection before wrapping it in a scrap of newspaper and placing it in the box. She'd have an estate sale first, maybe sell some of the stuff online and then pack up the rest and take it home with her. She studied a mermaid carved from teak, running her fingertip along the smooth flip of hair. Her nose tingled and she swiped the back of her hand across it.

Kayla had loved playing mermaids, and Kendall had humored her twin by playing with her even though she'd have rather been catching frogs at the river or riding her bike along the dirt paths crisscrossing the forest.

She'd been the tomboy, the tough twin—the twin who'd survived.

She rolled the mermaid into an ad for discount prescription drugs and tucked it into the box at her feet. Thirty minutes later, she sprayed some furniture polish on a rag and swiped it across the empty shelves of the cabinet. One down, two to go.

The round metal handle on the drawer clinked and Kendall groaned. Most likely, Aunt Cass had more stuff crammed into the drawer.

She curled her fingers around the handle and tugged it open. She blew out a breath—papers, not figurines.

Grabbing a handful, she held the papers up to the light. Bills and receipts. Probably of no use to anyone now.

She ducked and grabbed the plastic garbage bag, already half-full of junk she'd pulled from her aunt's desk. She dropped the papers in the bag, without even looking at them, and reached for another batch.

A flash of color amid all the black and white caught her eye, and her fingers scurried to the back of the drawer to retrieve the item. She tugged on a silky piece of material and held it up.

The pink ribbon danced from her fingertips, taunting her. She couldn't scream. She couldn't breathe.

She crumpled the ribbon in her fist and ran blindly for the door.

Chapter Two

Sheriff Cooper Sloane wheeled his patrol SUV onto
the gravel driveway of Cass Teagan's place, the damp
air tamping down any dust or debris that his tires even
considered kicking up.

He owed Wyatt Carson for giving him the heads-up
about Kendall Rush's presence at her aunt's house. The
plumber hadn't even done it on purpose, just let it slip.

He opened his car door and planted one booted foot
on the ground where it crunched the gravel. He clapped
his hat on his head and adjusted the equipment on his
belt.

As he took one step toward the house, the front door
crashed open and a woman flew down the steps, her
hair streaming behind her, a pair of dark eyes standing out in her pale face.

She ran right toward him, her gaze fixed on something beyond his shoulder, something only she could
see.

"Whoa, whoa." He spread his arms as she barreled
into him, staggered back and caught her around the
waist so she wouldn't take both of them down.

Her heart thundered against his chest, and her mouth

dropped open as one hand clawed at the sleeve of his jacket.

"Ma'am. Ma'am. What's the matter?"

She arched back, and her eyes finally focused on his face, tracked up to his hat and dropped to his badge. She blinked.

"Are you all right?" Her body slumped in his arms, and he placed his hands on her shoulders to steady her.

Then she squared those shoulders, and shoved one hand in the pocket of her jeans. A smile trembled on her lips. "I am so sorry."

"Nothing to be sorry about." He gave her a final squeeze before releasing her. "What happened in the house to send you out here like a bat outta hell?"

She wedged two trembling fingers against her temple and released a shaky laugh. "You're not going to believe it."

Raising one eyebrow, he cocked his head. "Try me."

"S-spider." She waved one arm behind her, the other hand still firmly tucked into her front pocket. "I have an irrational fear of spiders. I know it's ridiculous, but I guess that's why it's irrational. A big, brown one crawled across my hand. Freaked me out. I should've just killed the sucker. Now I don't know where he is. He could be anywhere in there."

As the words tumbled from her lying lips, he narrowed his eyes.

She trailed off and cleared her throat. "Anyway, I told you it was silly."

"We all have our phobias." He lifted one shoulder, and then extended his arms. "After that introduction, we should probably backtrack. I'm Sheriff Sloane."

"Kendall Rush, Sheriff. Nice to meet you. I'm Cass Teagan's niece, and I'm here to sell her place."

"I know. That's why I'm here." He gestured toward the front door, which yawned open behind the screen door that had banged back into place after Kendall's flight from the...spider. "Can I talk to you inside?"

"Of course."

She rubbed her arms as if noticing the chill in the soggy air for the first time.

When she didn't make a move, he said, "After you."

She spun on the toes of her sneakers and scuffed her feet toward the steps with as much enthusiasm as someone going to meet her greatest fear—and it had nothing to do with spiders.

He followed her, the sway of her hips in the tight denim making his mouth water—even though she was a liar.

She opened the screen door and turned suddenly. His gaze jumped to her face.

Her eyes widened for a nanosecond. Had she busted him? He didn't even know if she had a husband waiting on the other side of the threshold. The good citizens of Timberline probably could've told him, but that piece of information hadn't concerned him—before.

Standing against the screen door, she held it wide. "You first."

"Still afraid that spider's going to jump out at you?"

Her nostrils flared. "Better you than me."

Something had her spooked and she hadn't gotten over it yet.

He patted the weapon on his hip. "I got him covered if he does."

"Even I'd consider that overkill for a spider."

He brushed past her into the house, and a warm musky scent seeped into his pores. He had the ridiculous sensation that Kendall Rush was luring him into a trap—like a fly to a spider's web.

The dusty mustiness of the room closed around him, replacing the seductive smell of musk and even overpowering the pine scent from outside. His nose twitched and he sneezed.

"I'm sorry. I haven't had time to clean up ten months' worth of dust in here yet." She plucked a tissue from a box by the window and waved it at him.

"Why don't you open a couple of windows?" He scanned the room, cluttered with boxes of varying degrees of emptiness, his gaze zeroing in on a cabinet with an open drawer, papers scattered around it.

"There was a breeze this morning, and I thought opening the window would stir up the dust and make it worse." She walked backward to the cabinet and leaned against it, shutting the drawer with her hip in the process.

"Hope to trap him in there?"

A quick blush pulsed in her cheeks. "What?"

"The spider." He pointed to the cabinet she seemed to be trying to block with her slight frame. "It looks like you were going through that drawer when you discovered him."

The line of her jaw hardened. "I was going through the drawer, but the spider crawled on my hand while I was carrying one of the boxes."

He looked at the neat row of boxes, not one dropped in haste, and shrugged. If she wanted to continue lying to him about what gave her such a scare that she'd run headlong out of the house and into his arms, he'd leave it to her. He hadn't minded the introduction at all.

"If I happen to see him or any of his brethren, I'll introduce him to the bottom of my boot." He tipped his hat from his head and ran a hand through his hair. "Now, can I ask you a few questions, Ms. Rush?"

"All right, but I can't help you."

"That's a quick judgment when you haven't even heard the questions yet." He put his hat on the top of a box filled with books. "Is there someplace else we can talk so I don't have a sneezing fit?"

"I cleaned up the kitchen pretty thoroughly. Do you want something to drink while we talk?"

"Just water." He followed her into the kitchen, keeping his eyes on the back of her head this time, although the way her dark hair shimmered down her back was just as alluring as her other assets.

She cranked on the faucet and plucked a glass from an open cupboard. "That's one thing I miss about living in Timberline, maybe the only thing—the tap water. It's as good as anything in a bottle."

"It is." He took the glass from her and held it up to the light from the kitchen window. He then swirled it like a fine wine and took a sip.

She pulled a chair out from the small kitchen table stationed next to a side door that led to a plain cement patio. She perched on the edge, making it clear that she was ready to get this interview over with before it even started.

She kicked out the chair on the other side of the table. "Have a seat."

He placed his glass on the table and sank into the chair, stretched his legs to the side and pulled a note-pad from his pocket. "You obviously know I'm interested in asking you questions about the kidnapping of your sister."

She drummed her fingers on the table. "Did Wyatt Carson tell you I was out here?"

"No. I heard you'd arrived yesterday—just local gossip."

She rolled her eyes, apparently not believing his lie any more than he believed hers. "Okay. Ask away, but you're asking me about something that happened a long time ago."

"A traumatic event."

"Exactly, I've squished down a lot of those memories, and I'm not inclined to dredge them up."

"Even if they can help the Keaton and Douglas families today?"

"I don't believe they can." She flattened her hands on the table, her fingers splayed. "You can't seriously believe the two current kidnappings have anything to do with the Timberline Trio disappearances. What, some kidnapper has been lying dormant for twenty-five years and then up and decides to go another round?"

"I think there are some similarities." He hunched forward in his chair. "There are cases where a serial killer is active and then the killings just stop, sometimes because the killer goes to prison for some other crime. Then when he's paroled, he starts killing again."

"So you think the man who kidnapped my sister is on the loose and picking up where he left off over two decades ago?" She folded her hands in front of herself, and his gaze dropped to her white knuckles.

Before his action even registered in his brain, his hand shot out and he covered her clasped hands with one of his. "I'm sorry. I didn't mean to be so blunt."

"I'd rather you be truthful with me, Sheriff Sloane."

"Call me Coop. Everyone does." He slid his hand from hers. "I'd like you to be truthful with me, too, Ms. Rush."

Her eyes flickered. "Call me Kendall, and I'll be as truthful as I can. What do you want to ask me?"

So he wouldn't be tempted to touch her again, he dragged his notebook in front of him and tapped the eraser end of his pencil on the first page. "What do you remember about that night?"

"That's an open-ended question."

"Okay. Why were you and your sister spending the night at your aunt's house instead of your own?"

"If you read the case file, you know the answer to that question."

"You're not going to make this easy, are you?"

Tucking her hair behind one ear, she ran her tongue along her lower lip. "I'm trying to make it easy on you and save some time. A lot of that stuff is in the case file. I don't see the point in rehashing it with me."

"You're the therapist. You understand the importance of reliving memories, of telling someone else your version of events. Isn't that what therapists are supposed to do?" His lip curled despite his best efforts to keep his feelings about therapists on neutral ground.

"You're trying to psychoanalyze me?"

"I'm trying to see if you have anything to offer that

doesn't come through on a page written twenty-five years ago." He snorted. "Unless you're trying to tell me talk therapy doesn't work. Does it?"

She studied his face, staring into his eyes, her own dark and fathomless. Could she read the disdain he had for therapy? He'd brought up the therapy angle only to make her feel comfortable.

She tapped the table between them with her index finger. "Therapy is supposed to help the subject. You want me to start spilling my guts to help you, not to help myself."

He closed his eyes and pinched the bridge of his nose. God, he wished he was questioning Wyatt again and not this complicated woman.

The gesture must've elicited her pity because she started talking.

"Kayla and I were at Aunt Cass's that night because my parents were fighting again. Aunt Cass, my mother's sister, felt that my parents needed to work out their differences one-on-one and not in front of the kids."

"The police suspected your father of the kidnapping at first because of the fight."

"I didn't realize that at the time, of course, but that assumption was so ridiculous. I'd given a description of the kidnapper, and I would've recognized my dad, even in a mask. I suppose the police figured I was too traumatized to give an accurate description or I was protecting my father."

"What was your description, since the guy had a ski mask on?" He doodled in his notebook because Kendall had been right. All this info was in the case file.

"He was wearing a mask, gloves, and he was taller and heavier than my dad. That I could give them. Oh, and that he had a gravelly voice."

"He just said a few words, though, right? 'Get off' or 'let go'?"

She shifted her gaze away from him and dropped her lashes. "I'd grabbed on to his leg."

"Brave girl."

"It didn't stop him."

His eye twitched. Did she feel guilty because she didn't stop a grown man from kidnapping her twin?

"No surprise there."

Her dark eyes sparkled and she shrugged her shoulders.

"He took something from you, didn't he?"

"My twin sister. My innocence. My security. My mother's sanity. My family. Yeah, he took a lot."

He wanted to reach for her again and soothe the pain etched on her face, but he tapped his chin with the pencil instead. "Not that it can compare with any of those losses, but he also took a pink ribbon from your hair."

The color drained from Kendall's face, and a muscle quivered at the corner of her mouth.

"Do you want some water?" He pushed back from the table. "You look pale."

"I'm okay." Her chest rose and fell as she pulled in a long breath and released it. "I'd forgotten about that ribbon. Pink was Kayla's favorite color. Mine was green. That night Aunt Cass had put our hair in pigtails, and Kayla had insisted on tying pink ribbons in my hair while she tried the green. I was glad he took that ribbon."

"Why?" He held his breath as Kendall's eyes took on a faraway look.

"I always thought that when Kayla woke up and found herself with this strange man, she'd feel better seeing the pink ribbon. Now..." She covered her eyes with one hand.

"Now?" He almost whispered the word, his throat tight.

"Now I think that he just killed her, that she never saw the ribbon."

When her voice broke, he rose from his chair and crouched beside her. He took the hand she had resting on the table and rubbed it between both of his as if she needed warming up.

"I'm sorry. I'm sorry I'm forcing these memories and thoughts back to the surface."

A misty smile trembled on her lips. "This is exactly what I put my clients through every day."

"And it's supposed to help them. Is it helping you?"

Sniffling, she dabbed the end of her nose with her fingertips. "This is well-traveled territory. It's not like I haven't been through all of this before with my own therapist."

"You see a therapist?" He sat back on his heels.

"All therapists do at the beginning. It's part of our training, and most of us keep it up because it helps our work."

"So I must be a poor substitute." Although he could probably do a better job than half the quacks out there.

She curled her fingers around one of his hands. "She never holds my hand, so you've got her beat there."

He squeezed her fingers and released them as he

backed up to his own seat. "Did your therapy ever bring up any memories of that night that you hadn't realized as a child? The man's accent? Someone he reminded you of?"

"Nothing like that." She stretched her arms over her head. "I don't have any repressed memories of the event, if that's what you're driving at, Doctor Sloane."

He stroked his chin, wishing he had a clean shave. "You know, sometimes I feel more like a psychiatrist than a cop when I'm questioning people."

"So tell me." She wedged her elbows on the table and sunk her chin into one cupped palm. "What makes you think these two kidnappings are at all related to the Timberline Trio case? Wyatt mentioned you were working on some theory that the FBI didn't share."

When Kendall mentioned the FBI, he ground his back teeth together. He'd never met a more arrogant bunch, who seemed more interested in dotting *i*'s and crossing *t*'s than doing any real investigative work.

"It's something I'd rather keep to myself."

She swiped his glass from the table and jumped up from her chair. As she sauntered toward the sink, she glanced over her shoulder. "You want me to help you, but you won't share your findings?"

"Can you keep a secret?" He sucked in his bottom lip as he watched her refill his glass with water from the tap. She'd lured him into a comfortable intimacy, making him forget that she'd lied about the spider, but she seemed like someone who could keep secrets because she had plenty of her own.

"Who am I going to tell? I'm only going to be here

for a short time anyway. Pack up the house, list it, outta here."

He scooted back his chair and stood up, leaning his hip against the table. "When this guy snatched the two children on separate occasions, he left something behind."

"What?" She placed the glass on the counter and wiped her fingers on the dish towel hanging over the oven's handle.

"When he took the boy, he left a plastic dinosaur. When he took the girl, he left...a pink ribbon."

Chapter Three

The room tilted and Sheriff Sloane's handsome face blurred at the edges. The pink hair ribbon that she'd found in the drawer of the cabinet burned a hole in her pocket where she'd stuffed it.

What did this mean? Who had put the ribbon in the drawer? What was the significance of the ribbon left at the scene of the kidnapping?

She swallowed. "A dinosaur?"

"You didn't know that, did you?" He reached over and took the glass from the counter. "When Stevie Carson was kidnapped, his parents insisted that one of his dinosaurs from his collection was missing. When Harrison Keaton was taken from his bedroom, the same kind of dinosaur as Stevie's was on the floor."

"The boy's parents confirmed the dinosaur didn't belong to him...to Harrison?" She twisted her fingers in front of her.

He gulped down half of the water. "No. That's why the FBI isn't looking at this angle. Harrison's parents can't say whether the dinosaur belongs to him or not."

"And the p-pink ribbon?"

"Same thing. The ribbon was on the little girl's dresser. Cheri Douglas wears ribbons. She likes pink."

Kendall eked out a tiny breath. Sounded like a coincidence to her. Lots of little boys played with plastic dinosaurs. Lots of little girls wore ribbons, especially pink ones, in their hair. Sheriff Sloane was grasping at straws, perhaps trying to stay relevant as the FBI moved into Timberline and took over the investigation.

She hooked her thumb in the front pocket of her jeans, the ribbon tickling the end of her finger. "Your theory is a stretch."

"Could be." He downed the rest of the water. "I'll let you get back to work, Kendall. If anything comes to you while you're still in town, give me a call."

He plucked a white business card from the front pocket of his khaki shirt and held it out between two fingers.

Taking it from him, she glanced at the embossed letters before shoving it in her back pocket. "I'll do that."

"I'd appreciate it if you didn't mention the ribbon or dinosaur to anyone else—just in case they mean something."

"My lips are sealed. As a therapist, I'm good at keeping secrets. It's part of my job description."

"I figured you were, or I wouldn't have told you. I think you're probably very good at keeping secrets." He jerked his thumb toward the living room. "I'm gonna head on out."

She followed him into the other room and then scooted past him to open the front door. "It was nice meeting you, Sheriff Sloane—Coop. I sure hope you can help those families, and I wish I could do more."

"I appreciate your time, Kendall. I'll probably be seeing you around before you leave." He stopped on the porch and did a half turn. "Watch out for those... spiders."

She squinted through the heavy mesh of the screen door at the sheriff as he climbed into his SUV. He beeped his horn once as he backed down the drive.

He hadn't bought her story about the spider. She did hate the creepy crawlies, but that mad flight from the house would've been over-the-top even for her.

Shutting the door, she dug into her pocket, the ribbon twining around her fingers. She pulled it free and dangled it in front of herself.

The soft pink had a slight sheen to it that caught the lamplight. It couldn't be the same one yanked from her pigtail that night or even its companion. A twenty-five-year-old ribbon would be faded and frayed, not buoyantly dancing from her fingertips.

She dropped it on top of the cabinet and shuffled through the drawer where she'd found it. Nothing else jumped out at her, not even a spider.

Although the ribbon had spooked her, there was probably a good, reasonable explanation for its presence in the drawer—not that she could think of one now.

She grabbed another handful of papers and shoved them into the plastic garbage bag. The sooner she got Aunt Cass's place ready, the sooner she could get out of this soggy hellhole.

And the sooner she could escape the tragedies of Harrison and Cheri. Damn Sheriff Sloane for naming them and making them human—a boy who liked dinosaurs and a girl who liked pink hair ribbons.

And damn Sheriff Sloane for peeling back her facade so easily. He'd just given her another reason to run back to Phoenix.

A man like that spelled trouble.

A FEW HOURS LATER, Kendall scrubbed the grit and dust from her skin under the spray of a warm shower—her first since arriving in Timberline because she'd forgotten to contact the gas company until she got here. If she'd known she would be having a meet and greet with the hunky sheriff in town, she would've gotten on that sooner.

She'd been dreading the social engagement tonight but after finding that ribbon and answering the sheriff's prying questions, she was glad for the distraction.

Melissa Rhodes, a friend of hers from high school, had invited her over for a dinner party. Even if she didn't plan to stay in Timberline longer than she had to, she'd use the time to catch up with some old friends—the few that still remained.

The dinnertime conversation had better not revolve around the current kidnappings or she'd have to cut the evening short.

She stepped into a pair of skinny jeans and pulled some socks over the denim and finished off with knee-high boots. Topped with a sweater, the outfit pretty much defined the casual look for the Washington peninsula.

Her flip-flops and summer skirts called to her, but she hadn't even packed them for this cold climate.

She braided her long hair over one shoulder, brushed on a little makeup, and then yanked a wool shawl off the hook by the door.

Crossing her arms, she faced the living room and took a deep breath without worrying about choking on the dust for the first time since she'd arrived. After Sheriff Sloane had left, she'd gotten down and dirty with a rag and a can of furniture polish. She even took a vacuum to the drapes at the windows.

Rebecca, her Realtor, would be thrilled with the progress.

After locking up, she slid into her aunt's old truck and trundled down the drive to the main road. The lush forest hugged the asphalt on either side, the leaves still dripping moisture from the rain shower an hour ago.

The brakes on the truck had seen better days, and Kendall mentally added the sale of the vehicle to her list of to-do items. There had to be some local kids who wanted to practice their auto shop skills on an old beater.

She drove the few miles on slick roads and pulled behind a line of cars already parked on the street in front of Melissa's house—Melissa and Daryl's house. Daryl had come to Timberline almost two years ago to take a job with Evergreen Software and had fallen for a local girl. Melissa had never left Timberline since she'd had to take care of her mom who'd had Parkinson's disease. She'd found her prince charming anyway, in the form of a software engineer.

As she ground the gear shift into Park, Kendall winced. Anyone interested in this truck had better be a good mechanic.

She jumped from the truck and wrapped her shawl around her body as she headed up the pathway to the house. Warm lights shimmered from the windows and smoke puffed from the chimney.

She knocked on the door, tucking the bottle of cabernet under one arm.

A man—presumably Daryl—opened the front door and broke into an immediate smile. "You must be Kendall."

"I am." She stuck out her hand. "And you must be Daryl."

Taking her hand, he pulled her over the threshold. "Honey, Kendall's here."

Kendall's gaze shifted over his shoulder to the living room, and her fingers tightened around the neck of the bottle as several pairs of eyes focused on her. The few friends Melissa had mentioned looked like a full-scale party, and it seemed like she'd just interrupted their conversation.

She rolled her shoulders. She liked parties. She liked conversations—some topics better than others.

"I brought sustenance." Kendall held up the bottle of wine.

"We can always use more alcohol." Melissa broke away from a couple and approached Kendall, holding out her hands. "So good to see you, Kendall."

Kendall hooked her friend in a one-armed hug. "Same. You look great."

"And you look—" Melissa held her at arm's length "—tan. I'm so jealous. I'm as pale as ever."

"What do you expect when the sun shines maybe

three times a year, if you're lucky?" Kendall jerked her thumb over her shoulder at the damp outdoors.

"She's dissing our lovely, wet, depressing weather." Melissa held up the bottle to read the label. "But she's not snobby enough to dis our local wineries."

As Melissa peeled away from her side to put the wine in the kitchen, Kendall stepped down into the living room. She waved and nodded to a few familiar faces, shrugging off her shawl.

Melissa materialized behind her, a glass of wine in one hand. "This isn't yours. Is merlot okay?"

"Fine. The other stuff's for you and Daryl to drink later."

"Thanks. Let me take your shawl. We keep it warm in here." Daryl joined them, and Melissa patted her husband's arm. "Daryl's a transplant from LA. After two years, he's still not acclimated."

"Has my scatterbrained wife introduced you to everyone?" He went around the room, calling out names Kendall forgot two seconds later, until he named everyone there.

Melissa started carrying dishes to the dining room table, and Kendall broke away from the small talk to help her. The other guests' conversation had seemed guarded, anyway, and she'd bet anything they'd been talking about the kidnappings before her arrival.

Joining Melissa in the kitchen, she tapped a Crock-Pot of bubbling chili sitting on the kitchen counter. "Do you want this on the table, or are you going to leave it here?"

"You can put that on the table next to the grated cheese and diced onions."

Kendall hoisted the pot by its handles and inhaled the spicy aroma. "Mmm, this has to be your mom's recipe."

"It is." She patted the dining room table. "Right here."

Kendall placed the Crock-Pot on the tablecloth and removed the lid. "What else?"

"Can you help me scoop some tapenade and salsa and some other goodies into little serving dishes?"

"Absolutely, as long as I can sample while I'm scooping." Kendall pulled a small bowl toward herself and plopped a spoonful of guacamole in the center. "I like Daryl."

"Yeah, he's an uptight programmer—just perfect for his flaky, artsy-fartsy wife."

"Opposites do attract sometimes. He's a good balance for you."

"And what about you?" Melissa pinched her arm. "Any hot guys in hot Phoenix?"

"Lots, but nobody in particular. You single gals here in Timberline hit the jackpot when Evergreen Software came to town, didn't you?"

"It definitely expanded the dating scene, but a lot of the Evergreen employees came with ready-made families. Came to Washington for clean air, clean living, safety. Or at least it was safe until…" Melissa shoved a tapenade-topped cracker into her mouth.

"I know all about the recent kidnappings, Melissa." She scraped the rest of the guac into the bowl. "Wyatt Carson dropped by today and so did Sheriff Sloane."

"Coop already talked to you?"

"He came by the house this afternoon."

"Talk about your hot property." Melissa licked her fingers.

"He is definitely hot." Kendall elbowed her friend in the ribs. "I'd like to see him without all that khaki covering everything up."

"Ladies? Need any help?"

Kendall's face burned hotter than the salsa she was dumping into the bowl. She didn't have to turn around to know who'd crept up behind them. She'd been listening to that low-pitched, smooth voice all afternoon.

"Hey, Coop. Glad you could make it." Melissa nudged Kendall's foot with her bare toes. "Have you met Kendall Rush yet?"

Kendall got very busy wiping salsa spills from the counter as she glanced over her shoulder, trying not to zone in on the way the man's waffle knit shirt stretched across his broad chest. "We met this afternoon. Hello again, Sheriff Sloane."

"I thought we were on a first-name basis. Call me Coop."

He entered the kitchen with a few steps and, even though he still must've been yards behind her, it felt like he was breathing down her neck.

"Do you need any help in here, Melissa?"

"I do not. We have it all under control." She tapped Kendall's arm. "My hands are goopy. Can you grab a cold beer for Coop from the fridge?"

Kendall shuffled over a few steps and yanked open the refrigerator. "What kind would you like?"

"Anything in a bottle, not a can. Surprise me."

She studied the bottled beer, grateful for the cool air on her warm cheeks. Had he heard their schoolgirl conversation about him? She grabbed a bottle with a blue label and spun around, holding it up. "How's this?"

He ambled toward her, his eyes, as blue as the label on the bottle, sparkling with humor. He reached for the beer and for an electrifying second his fingertips brushed hers. With his gaze locked on hers, he said, "This'll do."

"Well, then." Melissa grabbed a dish towel and wiped her hands. "Once we get these bowls to the table, dinner will be served."

Coop reached around Kendall, his warm breath brushing her cheek, and pinched the edge of a serving dish between his fingers. "I'll get this one."

Kendall followed him to the dining room while Melissa made wide-eyed faces at her, which she had no idea how to interpret.

"Come and get it," Melissa called out to the group. "Paper plates and bowls on both sides of the table. Nothing but first class around here."

Coop stuck to her side as they both filled up plates and bowls with food.

Stopping at the chili, Kendall spooned some into her bowl and held up the ladle to Coop. "Have you tried Melissa's famous chili yet?"

"Nope. Fill 'er up."

She dipped the spoon into the dark red mixture and ladled it into his bowl. "Another?"

He nodded.

"This stuff only makes it better." She sprinkled some grated cheese, chopped onions and diced avocado on the top.

Holding her plate in one hand and a bowl in the

other, her fingers curled around her plastic cutlery, Kendall shuffled into the living room and nabbed a spot at a card table Melissa had set out for her guests. As she placed her food on the plastic tablecloth, Coop joined her.

"You left your wineglass in the kitchen. Do you want a refill?"

"I don't have far to drive, but I'm still driving. I'll take some iced tea. There are some cans in the fridge."

"Responsible driver." He put his fist over his heart. "Just what a man of the law wants to hear."

By the time Coop returned with their drinks, Melissa and Daryl had claimed the other two places at the table, but they didn't last long. One or the other and sometimes both kept hopping up to see to their guests' needs, which left Kendall alone with the sheriff...which suited her just fine.

"Verdict on the chili?" She poked the edge of his empty bowl with her fork.

"Awesome. I'm going to have to ask her for the recipe."

Blinking, she stole a glance at his ring finger, which she hadn't bothered to check before. Bare. She hadn't pegged him as a domestic sort of guy. Maybe he was joking about getting the recipe.

With his face all serious, he took a sip of the beer he'd been nursing all through dinner and started cutting into a piece of barbecued chicken.

"Did you have any more scares cleaning up your aunt's place after I left?"

Knots tightened in her gut, but she didn't know if

thinking about the pink ribbon had caused the sensation or the fact that Coop had nailed her as a liar.

"If you don't count the scary dust bunnies, all went smoothly. I'm going to hire a cleaning crew to come in and finish the rest of the house, so I can focus on selling my aunt's things."

"You're not taking any of it back home?"

"Aunt Cass's decorating style and mine clash." She slathered a pat of butter on a corn bread muffin and took a bite.

"She had a lot of collections, didn't she?"

"Mermaids, wood carvings from the old days when Timberline was a lumber town—stuff like that."

"And you're just going to sell that stuff? Might be nice to hand down to the kids one day."

She almost inhaled a few crumbs of corn bread. Kids? She had no intention of having kids. Ever. She coughed into her napkin. "Maybe."

He reached forward so suddenly, she jerked back, but then he touched his fingertip to the corner of her mouth. "Corn bread."

To quell the tingling sensation his touch had started on her lips, she pressed the napkin to her mouth again. "Great. Do I have chili in my eyebrows, too?"

Taking her chin between his fingers, he looked in her eyes, his own darkening to a deep blue. "Not that I can see."

Laughter burst from the crowd sitting on the floor around the oversize, square coffee table, startling them both. He dropped his hand.

"You heard that story, didn't you, Coop?" A woman from the group called to him.

He eased back into his chair and finished off the last of his beer. "What's that, Jen?"

"Davis Unger, the little boy in Ms. Maynard's class, who announced to everyone that his mom and the mailman were boyfriend and girlfriend."

Coop chuckled. "Out of the mouths of babes. Does Mr. Unger know about that relationship?"

"I think it was all a misunderstanding."

"Riight."

"Doesn't your daughter give you the kindergarten report every day?"

His daughter? Kendall sucked in a quick breath, her gaze darting to that finger on his left hand again.

"Steffi's in her own little world half the time." He stood up and stretched. "When I ask her about school, she tells me bizarre stories about unicorns and fairies. Should I be concerned?"

Jen and a few of the other women laughed. "She just has an active imagination, and all the kids are crazy about that fairy movie that just came out."

Coop piled up his trash, and his hand hovered over her mostly empty plate. "Are you done?"

"You don't need to wait on me." She pushed back from the table, crumpling her napkin into her plate. "After all that food, I need to move. Let me take your empties, and you can go over there and discuss kindergarten."

A vertical line flashed between his eyes as he handed his paper plate and bowl to her. "I'll do that."

"Another beer?"

"Wouldn't do for the sheriff to set a bad example, would it?"

"Not at all." She meandered back to the kitchen, exchanging a few words here and there with Melissa's guests.

She slipped the trash into a plastic garbage bag in the kitchen and cleaned up some other items from the counter. Maybe Coop was divorced and had joint custody with his ex. Melissa would know. She made it her business to know everyone else's.

But the interrogation would have to wait. Melissa took her hostessing duties very seriously, and Kendall couldn't get one word with her alone.

After chitchatting and helping out with the cleanup duty, Kendall checked the time on her phone and decided to call it a night. She had a meeting with Rebecca tomorrow morning and wanted to check out a few online auction sites to assess Aunt Cass's collections.

She eyed Coop across the room talking with a couple of men and mimicking throwing a football. Thank God she hadn't stuck her foot in her mouth and admitted to never, ever wanting children since Coop had one.

Not that Coop's parenthood, marital status or anything else about his personal life would matter to her one bit once she flew the coop. She grinned at her lame joke and strolled to the den off the foyer to grab her shawl.

She dipped next to Melissa sitting on the couch and whispered in her ear. "I'm going to take off. I'm exhausted."

"Are you sure? There's still dessert."

"I can't handle another bite, but let's try to get together for lunch before I leave."

"Let me see you out." Melissa rocked forward, and Daryl placed a hand on her back to help her up.

"Nice to meet you, Daryl. You and Mel are welcome in Phoenix anytime." She pecked him on the cheek, and he gave her a quick hug around the neck.

Melissa took her arm as they walked to the front door. "Daryl and I are taking off for Seattle for a few days, but we should be back before you leave. Don't be a stranger while you're here and if you need any help with Aunt Cass's house, call me."

"Call *you* for help cleaning a house?"

"Hey." Melissa nipped her side with her fingertips. "I know people."

"I think I know the same people."

Coop materialized behind Melissa. "I'll walk you to your truck."

With her back to Coop, Melissa gave her a broad wink.

"Okay, thanks." Kendall hugged her friend good-bye and stepped out onto the porch with Coop close behind her.

He lifted his face to the mist in the air. "Ahh, re-freshing."

"Are you a native of Washington?"

"No, California. I've been here about five years."

"Oh, the reviled California transplant."

He spread his arms. "That's me."

"Well, this is me." She kicked the tire of her aunt's truck.

He took her hand as if to shake it, but he just held it. "Good to talk to you tonight about...other things."

"It's always good to talk about other things." She squeezed his hand and disentangled her fingers from his.

She climbed into the truck and cranked the key twice to get the engine to turn over. Waving, she pulled into the street. As the truck tilted up the slight incline, an object in the truck bed shifted and hit the tailgate.

She drew her brows over her nose. She didn't have anything in the back.

She reversed into her previous parking spot and threw the truck into Park. As she hopped from the seat, Coop turned at the porch.

Using the light on her cell phone, she stood on her tiptoes to peer into the truck bed. She traced the beam along the inside where it picked up a bundle wrapped in a tarp. Then the light picked up one small, pale hand poking from the tarp.

Kendall screamed like she'd never stop.

Chapter Four

Kendall's scream pierced the still night and turned the blood in his veins to ice. Coop had already been making his way back down the drive when he'd heard Kendall's truck coming back to the house. Now his boots grappled for purchase against the soggy leaves on the walkway as he ran toward Kendall.

"What is it? What's wrong?" By the time he reached her, he was panting as if he'd just run a marathon.

She'd stumbled back from the truck and stood staring at the tailgate with wide, glassy eyes. Raising her arm, she pointed to the truck with her cell phone. She worked her jaw but couldn't form any words—no coherent words, anyway.

He pried the phone from her stiff fingers and aiming the light at the truck bed, he jumped on the bumper. The phone illuminated a light-colored tarp with something rolled up in it.

"I-it's a body."

His heart slammed against his rib cage when his gaze stumbled across a hand peeking from the tarp. He leaned in close, aiming the phone's flashlight at the pale appendage, sniffing the air.

He smelled...turpentine. The hard plastic of the hand gleamed under the light and he poked it with the corner of the phone.

Pinching a corner of the tarp between his fingers, he lifted it, exposing the foot of the mannequin.

He blew out a breath and jumped down from the truck. "It's not a body, Kendall. It's a mannequin."

Her eyebrows collided over her nose. "A mannequin?"

"Do you want to have a look?"

She hunched her shoulders and drew her shawl around her body. "No. What's it doing in my truck? I didn't put a mannequin in my truck. I don't even have a mannequin. Why is it wrapped up like that?"

"Beats me, but I'm going to get a few of my guys down here to collect some evidence, and I'd better call the FBI."

"FBI?" Her voice squeaked and she burrowed further into her shawl. "Why would you call the FBI?"

"I'm pretty sure the agents investigating the kidnappings will be interested in this development, or at least they should be."

"Why?" She tilted her head and her long braid almost reached her waist.

"The mannequin?" Coop chewed on his bottom lip before spitting out his next words. "It's a kid."

Kendall choked and swayed on her feet.

He jumped forward to grab her and ended up pulling her against his chest, wrapping his arms tightly around her shaking frame. Beads of moisture trembled in the strands of her hair, and he brushed his hand across the top of her head to sweep them off.

"Let's go inside. I'll make those calls and you can warm up." He rubbed her arms still wrapped in the shawl. "You're shivering."

"Do we have to?" she murmured against his chest. "You can't use your cell phone for those calls?"

"And keep you waiting around outside while I do? No way."

She placed her hands against his chest and leaned back, looking into his face. "I don't want to go back in there and make a scene. I'm surprised they didn't all come rushing out here when they heard me scream."

"They didn't hear you. I was standing on the porch and the decibel level is high in there. Someone even turned on some music, not to mention the house is set back from the street." He spread his arms. "So, no alarm bells."

"Until we walk into that house. They were already eyeing me in there like I was some kind of black cloud."

Grabbing the edges of her shawl, he tugged. "It's just a mannequin, Kendall, not a dead body. Just some kind of sick trick."

"If you really believe that, why are you calling out your officers, the FBI and God knows who else?"

"Because we've had two kidnappings in this town, and that mannequin was left for you. If there's any kind of forensic evidence in your truck, we need to get our hands on it."

"All right." She rolled back her shoulders. "Let's get this over with."

He ushered Kendall back into the house, but most of the guests were too busy talking, eating and singing karaoke in the corner to notice them.

As one of Daryl's colleagues from Evergreen hit a high note in a 1980s rock song, Coop winced and squeezed Kendall's arm.

She rewarded him with an answering grimace and an eye roll.

"Couldn't stay away from the karaoke?" Melissa sailed forward, snapping her fingers and shaking her hips. Then her eyes widened and the smile dropped from her lips. "What's wrong?"

Coop bent forward until his lips almost grazed Melissa's ear. "Someone pulled a prank on Kendall by leaving a mannequin wrapped in a tarp in the back of her truck."

"Why would someone do that?" Melissa clapped one hand over her mouth. "You think it has something to do with—" she glanced over her shoulder at her guests whooping it up "—the kidnappings?"

"Maybe, maybe not, but if it is just teenagers and we catch them, let's just say this could be a teachable moment for them."

"I'm sure that's all it is." She yanked on Kendall's braid and grabbed a phone from its stand. "You can use our landline. Our reception is so iffy down here, we can't always depend on our cell phones."

Coop called the station first and asked the sergeant on duty to bring a forensics kit and send a squad car over. Then he plucked Agent Dennis Maxfield's business card from his wallet and punched in his number.

While the phone rang, he covered the mouthpiece and jerked his chin toward an open bottle of wine on the counter. "Have another glass, Kendall. I'll give you a ride home when this is all over."

"Agent Maxfield."

"This is Sheriff Sloane. There was an incident tonight I thought you might want to know about. Someone wrapped a tarp around a child-sized mannequin and put it in a truck bed to make it look like a body."

"Sick SOB. What's that got to do with the kidnappings?"

Coop turned his back to Kendall and Melissa chatting over their wine. "The truck belonged to Kendall Rush."

Silence ticked by for two seconds. "Who?"

"Kendall Rush. Her sister Kayla Rush was one of the Timberline Trio."

"Yeah—twenty-five years ago."

Coop's jaw tightened. "It's a coincidence, don't you think? If the mannequin had appeared in some random employee's truck at Evergreen, I wouldn't be as interested in it as I am."

"Is your department already looking into it, Sheriff?"

"My guys are on the way."

"We'll let you handle…this one. Let us know if you find anything of interest to *our* case."

Coop had a death grip on the phone, but he closed his eyes and relaxed his muscles. "Copy that, Maxfield."

He held out the phone to Melissa. "Thanks."

"Well? Is everyone going to rush out here with their lights spinning and guns blazing?" Kendall swirled the single sip of wine left in her glass before downing it.

"Couple of my guys are going to have a look—fingerprints, fibers, footprints. Then they'll take the mannequin away and we can figure out where it and the tarp came from."

"My guests are going to know, aren't they?" Melissa's gaze slid to the merrymakers in the other room.

Coop snorted. "By the sound of it, they'll be too drunk to notice what's going on. I hope they all have designated drivers."

Ten minutes later, Sergeant Payton called to indicate he and the patrol officer were out front.

Coop popped a mini creampuff in his mouth and charged toward the front door, eager to escape the screeching duo on the makeshift stage.

"Hold your horses." Kendall grabbed on to his belt loop. "I'm coming with you."

"Are you sure?"

She covered her ears. "Even looking into the dead eyes of a mannequin has got to be better than this."

Nodding, he opened the door for her, releasing a breath into the cold night. The wine had done her good, or maybe it was being around people oblivious to her uneasiness. He glanced back into the room, still frothing with hilarity.

That wouldn't last long.

Both officers had double-parked their squad cars, since the party guests had left no room on the street. They broke off their conversation when Coop and Kendall exited the Rhodes' yard.

Sergeant Payton pushed off the door of his car and met them at the truck. "We already took a look. Creepy."

"Did you watch where you were stepping?" Coop

pointed at the ground. "Ms. Rush and I already tromped through here before we knew what we had."

The sergeant flicked on a spotlight to flood the truck bed and the area around it with light. "We had a look before, but either the person who planted the mannequin covered up any footprints and disturbances or the wind and rain did it."

Coop crouched next to the back tire and examined the road. It hadn't helped matters that Kendall had driven the truck away and then backed up. The moist dirt bordering the street showed no footprints except theirs.

The patrol officer joined them—a new kid named Quentin Stevens.

He held up a black case. "I have the fingerprint materials. Should I give it a try?"

"Why not? Dust the tailgate and all around the back of the truck."

"Do the homeowners have a surveillance camera, by any chance?" The sergeant poked his head into the yard.

"Not that I know of. Like I said, Ms. Rush and I were both attending a party at the house. The owners are friends of mine. I think they would've told me if they had cameras, but I'll ask."

The front door swung open, and a couple descended the porch steps. As they looked up, they stumbled to a stop.

"What's going on?"

Kendall cleared her throat. "Someone left something in my truck, probably a stupid joke."

The couple, who had two kids at home, picked up

their pace and approached the circle of white light. The woman spoke up. "What kind of joke?"

"A stupid mannequin."

The man draped his arm around his wife and forced a laugh. "Teenagers."

Coop shot a glance at his two deputies, willing them to keep quiet about the fact that the mannequin was a child and wrapped up to look like a dead body.

Melissa and Daryl must've ended the party because a steady stream of people started leaving their house, all drawn to the investigation area like lemmings to the sea.

Sergeant Payton and Stevens went about their business as Coop and Kendall fielded questions and kept the looky-loos at bay.

Finally, they all cleared out and when the last one drove off, Melissa and Daryl barreled down the drive.

Melissa took Kendall's hand. "Anything?"

"Nothing yet, but they're about to take the thing out of the truck."

"Maybe we'll find something when we bring it in." Coop opened the back door of the squad car. "Lay it in the backseat."

He turned to Daryl while the sergeant and Stevens wrestled with the mannequin. "Do you guys have a security camera on the house?"

"No, but after this? We're getting one. Tell us the best model to buy and we'll buy it."

"Will do."

"Sweetie, do you want to come inside for a while?" Melissa rubbed a circle on Kendall's back. "You're freezing, and I promise I won't make you help clean up—unless you want to."

"Thanks, Melissa, but I just want to get home."

Coop raised his hand. "I'm taking Kendall home."

"That's okay. I think that second glass of wine has worn off by now."

"Ha! Let me warn you, ma'am, if you attempt to get behind the wheel of this truck, I'm gonna have to arrest you."

Melissa squeezed Kendall's shoulder. "I can pick you up tomorrow, Kendall, to get the truck or if you want to leave the keys, Daryl can take it over in the morning."

"If you don't mind." Kendall dug the keys to the truck out of her purse and dangled them in front of Melissa.

Melissa snatched them from her fingers. "Not at all. Go—warm up, relax. You're in good hands with Sheriff Sloane."

They said their goodbyes and Coop bundled Kendall in the passenger seat of his civilian car—a truck but a newer model than Kendall's old jalopy.

He slid a glance at Kendall's profile, which looked carved from ice. "Are you okay?"

"I'm fine."

"It might just be a joke. There's some pretty sick humor out there, and you know teens."

"You're probably right. Why would the kidnapper want to expose himself to scrutiny before he collects his ransom?"

His hands tightened on the steering wheel in a spasm. She had to know that if the kidnapper hadn't demanded a ransom now, chances are good he never would. None was ever asked for her twin sister.

Spitting angry droplets against his windshield, the rain started up again before he pulled into her driveway. Steffi hated the rain and another pinprick of guilt needled him next to all the others for making her stay in a place she didn't like, a place that never seemed like home even though she was born here. It had seemed like a good idea at the time to stay. Now he wasn't quite so sure.

He parked the truck and killed the engine. He'd at least walk Kendall up to the front door, not that he felt comfortable leaving her here after that stunt.

She swung around. "Do you want to come inside for a minute? I hate the rain."

"Sure. This was supposed to be a relaxing evening for me, a kickoff to a few vacation days, and I spent the second half of it working."

"Sorry."

"I don't blame you—not much, anyway."

A smile quirked her lips, and she grabbed the door handle.

He exited the truck and followed her to the porch, scanning her outdoor lighting and the screens on her windows. She could use a surveillance system here, too.

She unlocked the door and twisted her head over her shoulder. "I think you'll find it a little easier to breathe in here compared to this afternoon."

He stepped across the threshold and took a deep breath. Not only did he not get a lungful of dust, but the sweet scent of a candle or some air freshener tickled his nose. "That's better."

"I can't vouch for the rest of the rooms, but at least this one's clean, and the kitchen and the bedroom where I'm sleeping." She tossed her purse on the nearest chair. "I'm going to admit defeat and get a cleaning crew in to finish the job."

"Probably not a bad idea." He poked the toe of his boot at one of the boxes. "When are you going to have the estate sale?"

"As early as this weekend. You looking for some furniture from the Nixon era?"

"I think I'll pass."

"Would you like something to drink?"

He took a turn around the room, his gaze wandering to the cabinet where the phantom spider had been hiding. "Coffee, if it's not too much trouble."

"None, but do you need to get home to your daughter?"

Ah, he knew that was coming. "She's having a sleepover with her friend, who happens to be the daughter of our receptionist at the station."

"She's five?" She crooked her finger. "Follow me to the kitchen while I make the coffee."

He folded his arms and wedged a shoulder against the doorway into the small kitchen. "Yeah, Steffi's five and a half, as she'll be quick to tell you, and she's in kindergarten at Carver Elementary."

"Good, old Carver." She poured water into the coffeemaker and punched the button to start the brew. "Are you...married?"

Knew that one was coming, too.

He held up his left hand and wiggled his fingers. "Nope."

"Divorced?"

Even though it had been business, he'd poked into her personal life and that intimacy must've given her the impression it was okay for her to return the favor. She probably wouldn't feel the same way if one of her clients turned the tables and started asking her personal questions.

"I'm sorry. I'm prying. Occupational hazard. You can just ignore me, if you like." She turned and grabbed the handle to the refrigerator. "Milk with your coffee? No cream."

"I take it black, and I don't mind the third degree."

"Yes, you do." She pulled a carton of milk from the fridge. "Your face closed down, and your mouth got tight."

"You'd be good interviewing suspects." He took a quick breath and then blurted out, "She's dead."

Her hand jerked and the milk she'd been pouring into a mug sloshed onto the counter. "Excuse me?"

"My wife—she's dead."

"I'm so sorry." She swiped a sponge from the sink and dabbed at the pool of milk.

He pointed to the coffeemaker, the last drips of coffee falling into the pot. "Coffee's done."

Kendall tossed the sponge back into the sink and poured a stream into his cup. Then she added some to the mug with the milk.

Taking the handles of both cups, she said, "Let's go sit in the living room where it's warmer."

He took the mug from her. "Thanks."

They sat in chairs across from each other, and he used the box next to his chair as an end table.

"Do you like Timberline?" She watched him over the rim of her cup and he got the sense that she had the same look in her eye when she was sitting across from a patient or a client or whatever term they used.

"I like it. I'm an outdoorsy kind of guy, so I like the fishing, hiking, rafting."

"You've come to the right place for that." She ran the tip of her finger around the rim of her mug. "Looks like Evergreen Software is making an impact on the area. Young and Sons Lumber had gone out of business before I left for college, and Timberline was in danger of becoming a ghost town."

"Evergreen had already planted stakes by the time I got here, so I don't have the before and after picture, except from the locals' stories of the old days, and Mayor Young is always crowing about how much he's done for development in Timberline."

"Ah, so Jordan Young is mayor now."

"Actually, he stepped down recently, but he's a one-man cheerleading squad."

"Timberline does have a storied history—from silver mining to lumber to high tech. It's nice to see some life in the old place—maybe a little too much life." She wrapped both hands around her mug. "What do you really think about that mannequin?"

He blew the steam from the surface of the coffee

in his cup and took a sip. "I don't think it was a coincidence that it was left for you, even if it was a joke. Everyone in town knows your connection to the old kidnappings."

"I wonder if Wyatt got any surprises tonight." She tapped her fingernail against her mug. "I'm not the only one in town connected to the Timberline Trio, although it's just the two of us after Heather Brice's family left the area. I don't suppose her older brother, wherever he is, has been getting these little reminders"

"Good idea. I'll check with Wyatt tomorrow. He's still working on a job at the station for us."

"I have a hard time believing it's the kidnapper who left it. What's the point?"

"He's a kidnapper. Who knows? There could be a million reasons in his deranged mind—if he has a deranged mind."

Her eyes widened. "It's like you just said—he's a kidnapper. Why wouldn't he have a deranged mind? Anyone who kidnaps a child for whatever reason has to be sick."

"These two kidnappings could be for a purpose."

"You mean like some kind of ring?" She laced her fingers around her cup as if trying to draw warmth from the liquid inside. "I can't bear to think about that possibility."

"I know. Believe me, as the father of a young daughter, I can't, either."

"Someone like that wouldn't hang around to plant mannequins in trucks."

"Exactly, so we don't know what we're looking at

yet, but I'm sure that mannequin is connected to the kidnappings, even if it is just a cruel joke on you."

She yawned and covered her mouth. "Sorry. Not even coffee can keep me awake after the day I've had."

"I'll get going. Didn't mean to keep you up all night."

His mind flashed on keeping her up all night another way and as her brows lifted slightly, he had an uneasy feeling the therapist could not only read his face but his mind, too—unless it was all an act. A therapist didn't know much more than a layman or a cop, for that matter.

"I was glad for the company. Having you here in this empty house made my jitters go away." She rose from the chair and held out her hand for his cup.

"Good." He handed her the mug. "Is it okay if I use your restroom before heading out?"

"First door on your right."

After he washed his hands and stepped into the short hallway, he heard clinking glass in the kitchen. He glanced at the cabinet again.

Something had spooked her this afternoon, and then the mannequin had spooked her tonight. Was this a pattern? And didn't he have an obligation to find out if it was?

He crept toward the cabinet and eased open the drawer, his gaze tracking through the contents.

"Shouldn't you get a search warrant before you go snooping through my stuff?"

Her cold voice stopped him in his tracks. Then he plucked the pink ribbon from the drawer and turned, dangling it in front of him.

"Funny-looking spider."

Chapter Five

Heat flashed across her cheeks and she dug her heels into the carpet to keep from launching herself at him and snatching the ribbon from his hand.

"Why are you pawing through my aunt's possessions? You can't wait for the yard sale?"

"Nice try, Kendall." He shook the ribbon at her. "This is what scared you this afternoon, sent you running for the hills."

"So what if it was?" She jutted her chin forward. "You're a cop, not my therapist. I don't have to reveal every facet of my life to you."

"I'd at least appreciate the ones that are pertinent to my case." He dropped the ribbon where it fluttered to the top of the cabinet.

"I didn't know it was."

"C'mon, Kendall, a pink ribbon like the one the kidnapper took from you that night? That's why it freaked you out, isn't it?"

She dropped her chin to her chest and studied his face through lowered lashes. "I'd just met you, so to speak. I felt foolish for taking off like that, for exposing my frailties to a stranger."

He wedged his hands on the cabinet behind him. "I can understand that, but why didn't you tell me about it tonight after you found the mannequin?"

"Not sure." She crossed her arms over her chest, cupping her elbows. "Telling you later would be admitting I lied to you."

"Look, Kendall." He blew out a breath. "You're right. You don't owe me anything. You don't even owe anything to those two grieving families."

She sliced her hand through the air. "It's not that I don't want to help them. God knows I do, but it can't be at the expense of my own mental health, especially if that help doesn't do anything to find their children."

"We don't know that yet. Let's put everything on the table." He launched off the cabinet and took her by the shoulders. "Trust me. Just trust me. Am I that scary? Do I come across as judgmental? I'm not."

She tilted her head back to look into his earnest blue eyes. Was it that important for him that he have her trust?

"You don't. Not at all." She ringed her fingers around his wrists, or at least as far as they would go. "I lied this afternoon because I didn't want you to see how affected I was by the events in my past, and I didn't think the ribbon had any meaning for the current case. I didn't tell you about the ribbon after the mannequin because it would've exposed my earlier lie. Is that plain enough for you?"

"Why try to hide your feelings about the tragedy? Anyone would be traumatized."

Her lips twisted into a smile. "Only the strong survive."

His eyes flickered for a second as they darkened with pain.

Who didn't trust whom here?

"You found the ribbon in the drawer of that cabinet. It can't be the same one." He jerked his thumb over his shoulder. "That's not a twenty-five-year-old ribbon."

She stepped back from his realm. How did he get truths from her so easily? Who was the therapist here?

"I've been thinking about it all day. It could be the original one left in my hair, or another one of Kayla's that my aunt found. If the ribbon hadn't been exposed to the sun, it wouldn't have faded. Or maybe my aunt had bought some new ribbons for some project, and this one happens to be pink."

"Or the same person who left a child-sized mannequin in your truck bed, left the ribbon for you to find knowing the effect it would have on you."

"Which brings us back to square one." She massaged her temples. "Why would the kidnapper, or anyone else for that matter, want to needle me?"

"Not sure, but it's on my list of things to find out." He skimmed a hand over his short hair. "It's late."

Hooking a finger on the edge of the curtain, she peeked outside. "The rain stopped—for now."

He touched her back. "Are you going to be okay?"

Turning, she curled her arm and flexed her biceps. "I'm tough. And, listen, I would've told you about the ribbon...eventually. Especially after finding the mannequin."

"I'm glad to hear that." He grabbed the handle and then turned his head to the side, so that she could see his face in profile only. "You don't have to be so tough, Kendall. I can share some of your burden. Let me."

Then he slipped outside, and she watched him until the darkness swallowed him.

If she transferred some of her pain onto his shoulders, it was only fair that he transfer some of his onto hers.

Because Sheriff Cooper Sloane had pain to spare.

"STOP KNOCKING YOURSELF OUT." Rebecca Geist, her Realtor, held out a card between two perfectly manicured nails. "I've used this cleaning crew before, and they're professional and reasonably priced."

"Thanks. I should've called them sooner." Kendall shoved the card beneath the phone on the kitchen counter. "But I did manage to get Aunt Cass's collections boxed up. I'm going to try to sell some of them at the estate sale, and I'm going to take the rest to one of those places that will list them online for a fee. I've already found a business in Port Angeles that will do that."

"Sounds like a good idea." Rebecca held up the camera hanging around her neck. "If we want to get this place listed, I need to take photos now. I can always replace them with newer photos once you clear out of here."

"This room, the kitchen, the master and the bathroom. Hold off on the other two rooms if you can until I get that cleaning crew out here."

"I think that'll be fine." She winked. "You know those buyers from California. They'll snap up anything in the low threes."

"Three hundred thousand dollars? This dump?" Kendall waved her arms around the small living room.

Rebecca put a finger to her glossed mouth and swiveled her head from side to side as if she suspected a potential buyer was lurking in the corner. "This," she said, spreading her arms, "is a charming cottage in the woods. Don't forget, you've got an acre of land here, and ever since Evergreen planted its corporate headquarters in Timberline the housing market—if not the weather—has been heating up."

"Okay, scratch that. It's a bucolic hideaway, a nature buff's paradise, a forest love nest." She could even half imagine that last one with the carpet stripped away, refinished hardwood floors, a Native American rug before a crackling fire in the grate—and Coop Sloane, half-naked, lounging in front of it.

One corner of Kendall's mouth curled up.

"That's the spirit." Rebecca nudged her side. "Of course, we will have to reveal the history of the house."

Kendall snapped out of her daydream. "History? Like when it was built and any additions? I can assure you, there have been no additions to this house."

"No, dear." Rebecca had the camera to her face and was aiming it around the room. "The kidnapping."

The daydream completely evaporated.

"Really? We have to reveal something that happened twenty-five years ago? It's not like the house is haunted." Her gaze darted around the room, bouncing over the cabinet with the pink ribbon stashed inside.

"Well, it *was* a crime scene, but I don't think the negative will be too great." Rebecca lowered the camera and chewed on her bottom lip. "Unless…"

"Unless what?"

"Unless the FBI can't solve these two current kidnappings, or God forbid, there's another. Then it might not just be your house, but the whole area that's going to suffer." Rebecca's cheeks flushed beneath her heavy makeup. "And the families. Of course, the housing market is nothing next to the pain of the families."

"That's a given. You don't have to explain yourself, Rebecca." Kendall twirled a lock of hair around her finger. "Hopefully, the FBI, along with Sheriff Sloane, can find the children and stop this guy."

"Mmm." Rebecca smacked her lips. "My money's on Coop. Have you met him yet?"

Kendall shoved a hand in her pocket, trying to look nonchalant. "I did meet him. We were at the Rhodes' party last night."

"Good-looking tough guy but has a sensitive side. How often do you get that combo?" She clicked her nails on the side of the camera. "Now that you brought up Melissa's party, what happened to your truck there? When I went to get coffee this morning at Common Grounds, someone was saying the cops were looking at your truck last night."

"Teenagers playing a prank."

"Little miscreants." She shivered. "Noah wants kids, but I told him I'd only agree if we can give them away before they hit puberty."

"Noah's your husband?" She tried to keep the hopeful note out of her voice, since it really shouldn't matter to her one way or the other if Rebecca Geist had any interest in Coop or not.

"Not yet, but we're working on it." She raised her

hand, wiggling her left ring finger. "He'll put a ring on it once we work out some little details."

Kendall raised her brows. "Sounds like a real estate deal instead of a marriage."

"Oh, yeah. That's one of the details. Noah wants me to sign a prenup, and I'm okay with it. He's loaded, already has one ex-wife and doesn't want another bleeding him dry."

"Sounds...reasonable."

"Works for us. I'm done in here." Rebecca pointed to the kitchen. "I'll take a few pics of the kitchen, the master bedroom and the bathroom, and then we'll head outside."

Kendall glanced at Rebecca's high heels. "You are *not* going back there wearing those. I can try to find you a pair of wellies, so you can slog around the moist earth or I can take the pictures for you."

Rebecca wrinkled her nose. "You are kind of rural out here, aren't you? If you wouldn't mind taking some pictures of the property out back, that would be great."

While Rebecca snapped away in the kitchen, Kendall headed to the bedroom and dug a pair of rain boots out of the closet. She toed off her sneakers and pulled the boots on over her bare feet, wiggling her toes.

"Bed made in here?" Rebecca poked her head into the bedroom.

"It's all yours." Kendall scuffed past Rebecca and lifted her jacket from the hook by the front door. She hadn't looked at the property that stretched beyond the patio since she'd been back. A small creek ran through it, but Aunt Cass had never done much with the land.

Rebecca emerged from the back rooms, lifting the

camera strap over her head. "I think those will work. Between you and me, if we get one of those California buyers in here with money to burn, they'll probably do a teardown. It's getting more and more common in this area since Evergreen went in. I hope you're not too sentimental about the place."

Sentimental? About a house that had a prominent role in all her nightmares? "Not at all."

"Good. You take this. It's just point and shoot." She snatched the camera back. "Although I should probably make a few adjustments for the outdoors."

"Follow me." Kendall stuffed her arms in the jacket and led the way to the kitchen where a door opened onto the property at the back of the house.

They stepped onto the cement patio, the edge of it dropping off to a small clearing before the trees and brush grew thicker. Kendall tilted her head back and flipped up her hood. "It's drizzling again."

"Big surprise." Rebecca tapped the camera's display screen while aiming it at the forest of trees. "Would be nice if you could get a shot of the creek. I plan on listing this as a waterfront property."

"All of Timberline is waterfront property." Kendall stuck out her tongue and caught a few raindrops in her mouth.

"Your turn." Rebecca thrust the camera at her. "Do you mind if I go back inside and, um, take some more notes."

"Be my guest. I have some sodas, coffee and tea bags in the kitchen. You'll have to warm up the coffee, but it should be fine."

"I still have my latte from Common Grounds, but I'll zap it in your microwave."

"How many pictures do you want?" Kendall ducked her head into the strap of the camera.

"Five or six. Use your judgment." Rebecca slipped back into the house through the door, leaving it open behind her.

Gripping the camera, Kendall crossed the patio and stepped off the cement where her boots squelched against the soggy leaves and saturated dirt. About halfway across the clearing, she turned and took a picture of the back of the house.

When the kidnapper had taken Kayla, he'd left by the front door, which led the police to suspect he wasn't a local, wasn't sure of the terrain back here—not that there weren't a few locals under suspicion.

A drop of rain had found its way into the neck of her jacket and ran down her chest. She shivered and drew the jacket closer. She snapped another photo as she neared the edge of the clearing and approached the dense forest.

The trees and bushes looked as if they presented a solid front, but her father had carved a path for Aunt Cass through the forest to the creek. Kendall parted the branches of some scrubby trees and the path materialized before her, somewhat overgrown, but still distinguishable if you knew where to look.

And she knew where to look.

Whenever her parents had brought her and Kayla to Aunt Cass's, Kendall would escape at the first opportunity to explore. She'd dragged her sister along a few times, but Kayla proved to be more of a hindrance than a companion.

Kendall bit her lip on the guilt. In exchange for having her sister by her side all these years, she would've gladly played with Barbies on the porch every day of her childhood, no matter how much the green mystery of the forest had beckoned.

The wind rustled the wet leaves and they whispered as if Kayla herself stood before her, laughing in disbelief of her twin's vow.

Kendall planted a booted foot on the path and allowed the branches to snap in place behind her. "You're wrong, Kayla. If I could've had you back, I'd gladly have dressed up dolls with you all day long."

Her voice sounded like a shout amid the stillness of the forest. Putting one foot in front of the other along the slick path, Kendall trudged down the slight incline to the creek.

The underbrush thinned out, and the sound of gurgling water broke the silence. She stepped on top of a fallen, rotting log, sending a colony of bugs scurrying out of their home.

She took a deep breath of the pine-scented air, and surveyed the creek. If it had ever run dry, she'd never seen it.

The camera hung heavy around her neck, reminding her of her purpose. She lifted it and positioned the viewfinder to encompass the creek and the big trees that bracketed a stretch of it.

That would be a good place to hang a hammock. Unfortunately, who would want to lounge under perpetually gray skies?

She pressed the button for the picture and scanned to the left. Her brows collided and she zoomed in on a couple of objects sticking up next to the creek bank.

Her heart pounded. Her skin tingled.

She dropped the camera where it banged against her midsection.

As if in a trance, she stumbled over rocks and twigs, her feet making a sucking sound as they met and released the saturated earth beneath them, her eyes focused on the bank of the creek.

When she reached the dreaded destination, that both drew and repelled her at once, she fell to her knees. Her hands shot forward and she traced the outlines of two crosses.

Two small crosses—just the right size for two children.

Chapter Six

"How long has she been out there?" Coop peered around the red-and-white-checked curtain at the kitchen door.

"Longer than I thought she'd be." Rebecca Geist swirled her to-go cup of coffee. "Long enough for me to almost finish my coffee."

"It's starting to come down again." He tapped on the glass of the window installed in the top of the door.

"It's been on and off all morning. I don't think she's going to get swept away by the creek, if that's what you're worried about."

"Maybe not, but that trail down to the water has to be overgrown. She might've tripped over a root or fallen tree." He zipped up his jacket over his khaki uniform. "I'm going to go find her."

"Go ahead, Sir Galahad."

"What?"

Rebecca wiggled her fingers at the door. "Go forth and rescue."

He rolled his eyes and yanked open the kitchen door. A few pieces of patio furniture huddled next to the house, under the eaves, as if trying to stay dry.

He marched past them, across the cement patio, and jumped into the dirt at the end of it. This would be a great place for a deck with a fire pit and a gas barbecue.

He slogged through the wet grass of the clearing until he hit the tree line. With gloved hands, he pawed at the branches bordering the forested area until he found the gap.

Broken twigs and mashed mulch marked Kendall's path down to the creek, and he followed in her footsteps. The silence of the forest closed around him, making him feel like the last man on earth.

"Kendall!" He called her name just to upset the stillness.

But she didn't answer.

Unease nibbled at the corners of his mind, and he lengthened his stride in an effort to suppress the worry. The tree stump came out of nowhere and he sprawled forward, the moistness of the dirt soaking into the knees of his pants.

"Damn!"

Staggering to his feet, he brushed the debris from his knees and lunged forward. By the time the world lightened up, his breath was coming in short spurts. He crashed into the clearing fronting the creek, and his mouth dropped open.

"Kendall!"

The frantic creature on the bank of the creek didn't even look up from her task—and her task was digging a hole with her bare hands.

He jogged toward her, tree stumps be damned, and called her name again.

This time she turned her pale face to him, and his

heart jumped into his throat as he stumbled to a stop. Her eyes resembled two dark pools, wide and unseeing.

Without saying a word, she resumed her digging.

He rushed to her side and almost bowled her over when he saw the two wooden crosses in front of her.

"Kendall, Kendall, stop." He crouched beside her and grabbed her dirt-caked hands formed into claws.

"Th-they might be here. The children might be here." Her voice broke into a wail.

He pulled her against his chest, and they both fell over, their heads inches from the roiling water of the creek.

"Shh. Kendall, let's get back to the house. Let's get you warmed up." He struggled into a sitting position, dragging her with him. "I'm going to call the FBI to take a look and finish the digging. You don't want to compromise any evidence."

She blinked and a rivulet of water ran down her cheek, and he couldn't tell if it was a tear or just the damned, unstoppable rain.

Hoisting himself to his feet, he hooked an arm around her waist to pull her up with him. "Let's go back."

With one arm around Kendall, Coop fumbled for his cell phone but as soon as the dark canopy of trees sucked them in, he lost reception. "I'll call when we get to the house. How are you holding up?"

Spreading her dirty palms in front of her, she dropped her head. "D-do you think that's where he buried them? Why? Why on my property?"

"We don't know anything yet, Kendall." He brushed a hand across her damp hair, and then flicked up her hood. "Even if the FBI wasn't interested in that mannequin last night, I'm sure Agent Maxfield will be all over this."

They tromped through the dark woods, which had taken on an even more menacing air. When Kendall's sister had been snatched, the FBI must've combed through this area. But they'd never found Kayla, Stevie or Heather. How did children just disappear off the face of the earth? It was every parent's worst nightmare.

The clearing of the house's backyard beckoned beyond the branches crisscrossing over the entrance to the pathway. Coop clawed his way through with one hand, never releasing his hold on Kendall since he still didn't believe her capable of standing on her own.

As they broke free of the underbrush, Rebecca called from the kitchen doorway. "Everything okay?"

Coop pressed his lips together and navigated Kendall to the patio. "Rebecca, can you run a warm bath for Kendall?"

"No!" Kendall dug her fingers into the arm of his jacket. "I want to know what's out there."

Rebecca put a hand to her throat. "What's wrong? What happened out there, Kendall?"

"There are two wooden crosses by the creek, two small crosses."

"You don't think…" Rebecca's eye twitched and she sat down—hard.

"We don't know what to think yet." He reached for the landline. "Did you notice crosses or anything else out there when you looked at the house before?"

"I never actually looked at the property, never went down to the creek. Just looked at the land surveys, property boundaries and some pictures." Rebecca's hand shot out, and she tugged on Kendall's sleeve. "What happened to you? Why are you so filthy?"

He held up his finger as the phone on the other end of the line rang. Agent Maxfield picked up on the third ring. Coop gave all the details to Maxfield and ended the call.

Kendall dragged her sleeve across her nose. "I saw those crosses, and I just started digging."

"Kendall, no." Rebecca jumped from the chair. "I'm going to get you some hot tea. Even if you won't take a bath, why don't you clean up in the bathroom?"

Kendall gazed at her mud-caked hands again as if they belonged to a stranger. "Is Agent Maxfield coming?"

"He's on his way with a team. Wash your face and hands and drink that tea."

Kendall pulled off her muddy boots and lined them up next to the door. Then she slipped the camera from around her neck and placed it on the kitchen table. "I hope I didn't ruin your camera."

"We'll worry about that later." Rebecca held a tea kettle beneath the tap.

When Kendall left the kitchen, Rebecca lifted her eyebrows at him. "Is she okay? It seems like she's in shock—not that I blame her."

"When I found her, she was on her knees digging into the ground with her bare hands." Coop scratched his jaw. "Looked like she'd lost it."

"Yeah, well I would've, too, after what she's been through." Rebecca plucked a tea bag from a tin canister by the stove and swung it around her finger. "If those kids are buried out there, I think we can say goodbye to a sale for a while."

"Really?" Crossing his arms, Coop tilted his head to one side.

"Just thinking ahead. Of course, that's not my only concern or even my primary concern." She dropped the tea bag into the mug and grabbed the handle of the kettle when it started whistling.

Kendall shuffled back into the kitchen in stocking feet, her hands clean, her face still smudged with dirt.

"You look somewhat human—" Rebecca trailed her fingers in the air "—but you really need to get out of those wet clothes."

Kendall took the cup Rebecca extended to her. "I had a jacket on. My clothes are not as wet as they look."

"Sit down, Kendall." Coop shoved out a chair with the toe of his boot. "Agent Maxfield and his guys will be here soon. They're staying one town over."

Her gaze traveled to the window in the back door as she curled her fingers around the mug handle. "I want to be there when they dig."

"Kendall." He pinched the bridge of his nose, squeezing his eyes closed. "I don't think that's necessary."

"It's my property, my…life. I want to be there."

"Do you mind if I don't?" Rebecca hitched her purse over her shoulder and grabbed the camera. "I'm going to get these pictures developed, list the house on MLS and put it up on my website—before anything else happens."

"You might want to tweak a few of those pictures

with a photo editor." Kendall dredged the tea bag up and down in the steaming water.

"Why?"

"That's when I first noticed those crosses—through the viewfinder on the camera."

Rebecca gasped. "That's just creepy. Thanks for the heads-up."

"I'm going to want to have a look at your pictures, Rebecca, so send them to me when you upload them to your computer." Coop pushed off the counter. "I'll walk you to your car."

He unfurled one of Kendall's umbrellas stashed in a wicker holder by the front door and held the screen open for Rebecca. Holding the umbrella over Rebecca's head, he accompanied her to her pearl-white caddy and stayed put while she fumbled at the driver's side door.

When she dropped onto the seat, she turned a pale face toward him. "You'll let me know, won't you? What they find?"

"Sure, I'll tell you, but if those kids are there, I won't have to. That news is going to spread around the town like a wildfire."

"I hope to God they're not. For Kendall's sake and the families', I hope to God they're not." Her voice quavered.

And this time, he didn't think Rebecca had the housing market on her mind. He slammed her car door and hustled back to the house.

Kendall was still sipping her tea, staring out the window. Her eyes had lost their vacant look, but he didn't like what had replaced it—fear, sadness.

"Are you okay? I'm going to make a few phone calls to the station."

"I'm fine. Go ahead." She dragged in a deep breath. "I'm not going to fall apart, despite what you witnessed out there."

"There are different ways to fall apart, Kendall."

"You're talking to a therapist here. I realize that. I'm not going to fall apart in any way."

He held up his phone. "I'm going to call the station, even though I don't think we can spare anyone to come out and assist the FBI."

"I thought you were taking a few days off, starting today."

"I have vacation time to burn, but I had to come in today—and now I'm glad I did."

"I know you have a small department, but was this section of the woods searched when the first child went missing?"

"Of course. We searched all along the creeks and rivers."

"So, those crosses are a recent addition to the landscape."

"It would seem so." He placed his cell on the counter and punched in the number to the station on Kendall's landline. The desk sergeant picked up on the first ring. Must be a slow day—in some parts.

"Anyone available to come out here, Sarge?"

"Probably not, Coop. Ever since the kidnappings, the folks want to see the police presence. We've got two guys on patrol right now."

"Okay, just keep everyone apprised of the situation, and I'm going to stay out here to wait for the FBI." He ended the conversation with the sergeant and placed two more calls. By the time he was off the phone, Kendall had finished her tea and had wandered into the living room.

She called out. "I think the FBI's here."

Coop joined her in the other room and looked out the window at the dark sedan pulling into the drive behind Kendall's truck. A white, unmarked van drove up seconds later.

Coop opened the front door and stepped onto the porch.

Maxfield started up the drive toward the house and Coop called out, "We'll meet you around the back. Go through the wooden gate to your right."

He shut the door and turned to Kendall. "You sure you want to do this?"

She answered him by yanking her still-damp jacket from the hook.

She pulled on her rain boots by the door and he followed her out to the cement slab her aunt had called a patio.

Agent Maxfield and another dark-suited agent with a trench coat led a procession of CSI types, two of them carrying shovels.

Coop's gaze dropped to the fibbies' dark wing tips, and he shook his head. At heart the agents were a bunch of city-boy desk jockeys.

"Let's do this, Sheriff Sloane. Lead the way."

After a few brief introductions, Kendall charged ahead. "I'll show you. This way."

The small army crashed through the wooded area,

dispelling the aura of mystery and foreboding he'd sensed before.

They swarmed into the clearing by the creek, and Kendall jabbed her finger in the air. "Over there."

As Maxfield drew closer to the crosses, he cursed. "Why is the area disturbed? Is this how you found it, Ms. Rush?"

"I disturbed it. When I saw the crosses, my first instinct was to dig."

"Was it?" Maxfield's nostrils flared. "Did you notice anything on top of the gra…ground?

"I didn't notice anything."

"Doesn't mean there wasn't something, and you disturbed it."

"Hey." Coop held up his hand. "Kendall was in shock. She reacted. Now let's move forward and make the best of what could be a terrible situation."

Kendall scowled at him for his efforts, and he rolled his shoulders.

"Hendricks, Wong, start digging—very carefully. Chafee, pull up those crosses and wrap them in plastic."

The agents got to work, and with each shovelful of dirt wrenched from the ground, Kendall sidled closer and closer to Coop.

Until her shoulder pressed against his.

The rain had stopped, but the soggy ground made for easy digging, and the agents barely broke a sweat as they piled up mud on the edge of the creek.

After one vigorous plunge into the earth, Kendall jumped. "Be careful, just in case…"

Maxfield responded. "Don't worry, Ms. Rush.

They're being as gentle as possible and examining every shovelful of dirt as they dump it out."

Kendall's body grew tauter and tauter with each passing minute. She was practically vibrating beside him, so he draped an arm across her shoulders and pulled her closer until every line of her body pressed against his.

"Maybe it's nothing at all, Kendall. Maybe someone planted two crosses by the river and there's nothing beneath them. Maybe it's a pet."

"Two pets?"

"Hey, hey, I got something." Wong waved his gloved hand in the air.

Kendall sprang from Coop's side as if she'd been poised on coils ready to launch.

Coop followed her with a knot in his stomach and a prayer on his lips.

Maxfield stepped in front of her, his arms spread out to the side. "Hold on, Ms. Rush."

"What is it?" She bobbed her head back and forth like a boxer, trying to see around Mayfield's body.

Coop could see over Maxfield's head, and Wong was plowing through a mound of dirt in his shovel with one hand.

"It's a box, a small, metal box." Wong held it up, and the gray of the legal-envelope-sized box matched the dreary sky.

Kendall let out a sob and stumbled backward, her body going limp.

Coop caught her against his chest and murmured in her ear. "It's a box—a small box. Just a small box."

Not nearly big enough to accommodate a child.

Mayfield held out his hand for the box. "Keep digging, Hendricks."

Wong smacked the box into his boss's palm. "Should I keep digging?"

"You can go a little deeper, but I think this is it."

But both agents had stopped their activity once Maxfield had the box in his hands. He began to pry open the lid carefully with his gloved fingers, and everyone seemed to stop breathing. The air pulsed with expectation.

Maxfield removed the lid. A white rectangle rested at the bottom of the box.

"Is it a note?" Kendall's voice held a hint of dread, and Coop wrapped his arms around her waist, his desire to shield her overpowering.

The object seemed to have mesmerized everyone. Coop cleared his throat. "I think it's a photograph. Maxfield?"

"I think you're right." He withdrew a leather case from his jacket, unzipped the case and selected a pair of tweezers from the felt-lined interior. He pulled off one glove to manipulate the tweezers and pinched the corner of the picture between the pincers and turned it over.

All six of the people in the circle recoiled, and Kendall cried out and dug her fist against her mouth.

"It's the girl, Cherie." Maxfield released the picture so that it dropped back against the metal box. "It's the girl holding a newspaper—proof of life."

"No, no." Kendall raked her fingers through her wet,

tangled hair. "It's not proof of life. The newspaper she's holding is from twenty-five years ago. The headline is for the missing Timberline Trio."

Chapter Seven

If Coop, solid as a rock, hadn't been behind her at those mini grave sites, she would've collapsed in the mud.

The other agent, Hendricks, had made a similar discovery under his cross, only the picture in the metal box had been that of the kidnapped boy, Harrison, holding another newspaper from twenty-five years ago with the Timberline Trio story.

The remaining FBI guy in her kitchen, Agent Maxfield, pocketed his phone and placed his coffee cup in the sink. "The parents are going to meet us at our hotel suite to look at the pictures. This development has given them a ray of hope."

Kendall swallowed and exchanged a look with Coop. She wouldn't exactly call finding pictures of the kidnapped children buried in graves with crosses stuck in the ground a ray of hope, but she understood the parents would be grateful for any shred of evidence that their children hadn't been immediately murdered. She hunched her shoulders against the shiver zipping up her spine.

Coop ended his own call to the station and asked,

"All the other evidence, including the pictures, is going to a lab?"

"We got this, Sloane."

Coop's jaw tightened. "The guy used a Polaroid camera to avoid having the pictures on his cell phone or having them printed out somewhere, but that in itself is a clue. Who still has a Polaroid camera these days?"

Maxfield shrugged. "Good question. I haven't seen one used in years."

Coop narrowed his eyes. "Now do you believe that mannequin in Kendall's truck is connected to the kidnapper? Those pictures were buried on her property for a reason."

"Maybe, maybe not. Maybe the reason was the soft earth next to the creek, the out-of-the-way location and the fact that the property had been vacant until Ms. Rush arrived yesterday."

Coop opened his mouth, and then shook his head. "Yeah, whatever."

"Thank you for the coffee, Ms. Rush. I know it was a shock for you to find those crosses on your land, but this is a big break for us."

"I—I hope it gives some comfort to the parents, and I hope it means those kids are alive."

She grimaced. But for what purpose if not ransom?

"I'm going to get back to our command center at the hotel and meet with the parents." He thrust out his hand. "Sheriff Sloane, thanks for your assistance. I can see myself out, ma'am."

She walked Agent Maxfield to the door anyway and

locked it behind him. Then she turned and pressed her back against it, closing her eyes.

She heard Coop's footfall on the carpet, and her eyelids flew open.

He took her hands. "Are you ready to get cleaned up now?"

She glanced down at her dirty clothes and stringy hair. "I guess so. You'd better head back to the station. You've been camped out here all day."

"For good reason. You heard Captain Obvious there. This is the biggest break they've had in the case yet— the only break. My guys know where I am and how to reach me—and technically I'm on vacation."

"I just hope it means Cheri and Harrison are safe… somewhere." She'd avoided using their names before, but they deserved to be human. Her bottom lip started to quiver and she sucked it in. "Anyway, thanks for all your help today."

"I'm off duty now. Well, I'm never really off duty, but I'm not expected back at the station today." He squeezed her hands once and released them. "You go take that bath that you should've taken about two hours ago, and I'll clean up the mess those fibbies made in your kitchen."

"You don't have to stay, Coop, really. I'm fine." Maybe she would've been more convincing if her voice hadn't wavered on the last word. She cleared her throat. "After seeing those crosses, I understand if you want to see Steffi, give her a hug."

"As a parent, seeing something like that gets you right here." He thumped his chest with his fist. "But somehow, I don't think Steffi would appreciate it if I came by her classroom and gave her a hug. And right after school she has a Brownie meeting."

"Okay, but if you have something to do, I'll be fine."

"I know *you're* fine, but I still need some time to decompress before I see Steffi later, and nothing says decompression like washing dishes."

"Right." She'd put up a fight, but she could tell by the set of his strong jaw that he wasn't about to leave her.

And she didn't want him to.

"The dishes are all yours, but lunch is on me."

He waved her off and strode toward the kitchen—a man on a mission.

She gathered some clean clothes from her bedroom and shut the bathroom door behind her. She turned on the water and shoved the plastic cherry-dotted shower curtain to one side.

The pile of dirty clothes mounted in the corner as she shed one damp layer after another. The clothes didn't even belong in the hamper with her other clothes. She didn't want to contaminate them with creek mud.

She stepped into the tub and faced the spray of water, scrubbing her body hard enough to remove a layer of skin. What was she trying to wash away, the terror of seeing those crosses or the years' old memories that still haunted her?

She poked her head around the shower curtain and grabbed a small brush from the metal caddy hanging above the toilet. She squeezed some soap onto the brush and scrubbed the dirt from her fingernails. She had no idea what she'd been trying to accomplish out there in the rain, on her hands and knees. Instinct had taken over with fear prodding her.

The tap on the bathroom door made her drop the brush.

"You okay in there?"

Coop was really worried about her. What did he think she'd do?

"I'm good. Just trying to get the last bits of dirt from beneath my fingernails." She ducked down to pick up the brush.

"Hurry up. Lunch is getting cold."

She shut off the water. "Lunch? I told you I would make lunch."

"I was too hungry to wait."

She yanked her towel from the rack. That man sure liked to take charge, but right now she didn't mind.

It took her ten minutes tops to dry off, shimmy into a pair of black leggings, a camisole and an oversize red flannel shirt. She stuffed her feet into a pair of fuzzy slippers and scuffed into the living room, still toweling off her hair.

Coop peered around the corner of the kitchen. "It's about time. I thought you'd gone down the drain."

He'd kept his tone light, but it still carried an edge of concern. Did he hover over his daughter, Steffi, like this, too?

"What's for lunch?" She bent over at the waist and wrapped the towel around her head in a turban.

"Get in here and see." He ushered her into the kitchen waving a checkered dish towel and then slung it over his shoulder.

She sniffed the air as she joined him in the kitchen. "Smells good and toasty—and like bacon."

"It's all of the above." He pulled out a chair from the kitchen table. "Grilled cheese with bacon and some tomato soup. You had the can of soup in the cupboard, so I assumed you like tomato soup."

"I do." She sat down and dropped the paper towel that was doubling as a napkin into her lap. "And this sandwich looks yummy. I feel like I'm back in grade school and coming home for lunch. Is this what you feed your daughter?"

"She doesn't like tomato soup, just chicken noodle or excuse me, chicken and stars."

"Sounds like a girl who knows her mind."

He rolled his eyes as he took the seat across from her. "If that's a euphemism for *stubborn*, yeah, she knows her mind."

Coop had even sliced the sandwich diagonally, and she picked up one half and bit off the corner. The melted cheese paired with the crunch of the bread with just a hint of butter fired up memories of warm hugs from Aunt Cass trying to comfort her, trying to make her feel whole again. The kidnapper hadn't just snatched Kayla from the family, he'd destroyed the family. Her father died too early, and her mother had a breakdown. Cass had been there though, maybe to make up for the guilt she'd felt that Kayla had been taken while in her care.

"Bread too soggy?" Coop's eyebrows rose over anxious eyes. "You stopped chewing."

"It's perfect." She dropped the sandwich on the plate

and brushed the crumbs from her fingertips. "The cheese is a little hot."

"When you were taking so long in the shower, I zapped everything in the microwave." He dipped his spoon in his bowl. "Are you warm enough? I was going to get a fire going in the fireplace, but I wasn't sure it was safe. If your aunt hadn't used the fireplace in a while, the chimney might need clearing."

"I'm not sure. The furnace works great, though, and I'm plenty warm." She swirled the tip of her spoon in the creamy, red soup, sending rings out to the edge of the bowl. "Do you think this kidnapper is the same guy who took my sister and the other two children?"

He took a big bite of his sandwich and took his time chewing. After he swallowed, he took a sip of soup. "He could be, although the gap in time is unusual."

"At least you're entertaining the thought, unlike the FBI."

"If he's not the same guy, this kidnapper is obviously aware of the Timberline Trio and is playing some kind of game." He tapped his spoon on the side of the bowl. "There might be three perps—the original kidnapper, the current kidnapper and someone else playing games. So, the one playing the games may not even be the kidnapper."

"How could he not be, after those pictures?"

"The pictures do suggest he's the same guy, but I'm not sure why the kidnapper would risk pulling these pranks."

"Didn't you just tell me last night that he was a kidnapper and we couldn't possibly guess his motives?

"I did say that, didn't I? I just can't figure out why

this guy is running around leaving hints that exponentially increase his chances of slipping up and getting caught." He slurped a spoonful of soup, and two red spots that matched the liquid in his bowl stained his cheeks. "Sorry for the noisy eating. That was hotter than I expected. I'm just glad Steffi didn't witness those bad manners since I'm always on her about stuff like that."

"Sounds like you're a good dad—grilled cheese sandwiches and good manners."

"I try."

She broke off a piece of crust from her sandwich. "How old was she when her mom died?"

Coop dropped his spoon in his bowl and took a long drink of water.

Was he going to refuse to answer? He must still be in love with his dead wife since he was so clearly not over the tragedy. She had a client in a similar situation—widowed six years yet had refused to date since. Of course, unless Coop answered, Kendall had no idea when his wife died. It could've been only months ago.

If so, she might have to shelve any designs she'd had on Cooper Sloane's body.

He finished off his water and swiped a paper towel across his mouth. "Steffi's mother died when Steffi was almost two years old."

Kendall was no math genius but she quickly figured three years should be plenty of time to move on, but as a therapist, she knew there was no one-size-fits-all for grief, and leaving a small child behind made healing even more difficult.

"I'm sorry, Coop."

"Thanks." He crumpled the paper towel and tossed it in his plate. "Do you need anything else before I take off?"

Had she driven him off with her questions? Her gaze darted to the back door. Of course, he had to leave at some point, but she wasn't ready to be in this house alone.

"I'm okay. I'm going to call the cleaning crew Rebecca recommended and post the estate sale online. I might even get ambitious and make a few signs."

"Sounds like you have your work cut out for you. I'm going to swing by the station before I head home." He stood up and took her dishes. "I know you're only going to be here for another week or two, Kendall, but maybe you should set up a security system—at least some cameras on the property. It'll be a good selling point for the house, even if you can't take advantage of it for very long."

"I like that idea. Where would I shop for something like that, a hardware store?"

"I'll help you out with it. I may be able to get it done for free since it could be a police matter."

"Free is good." She joined him at the sink and cinched her fingers around his wrist. "Stop washing. You already cleaned up after the agents and made lunch."

His strong hands stopped their busy work. "Then I'll leave it for you."

She handed him a dish towel to dry his hands. "Thanks for everything today, Coop, not just the cleanup and the lunch. I don't know if I could've handled finding those crosses on my own."

"Anytime." He took her by the shoulders, his touch at once gentle and insistent. "Just promise me one thing, Kendall."

When he looked at her with the intensity of those blue eyes, she'd promise him anything. Her lashes fluttered. "What?"

"If you ever feel scared or upset or…depressed, call me. Can you do that?"

Depressed? Despite the issues she carried with her from childhood, she rarely felt depressed. Had she presented as depressed? "I will. Thanks for the offer, but are you implying that a therapist shouldn't try to heal herself? Because we don't."

"Do therapists really *heal* anyone?" He'd kept his tone light, but something flickered in his eyes.

"*Heal* isn't the right word. I was just playing on the phrase 'Doctor, heal thyself.' As I told you before, a therapist isn't necessarily in therapy because they have issues."

"Do you? Have issues you need to work out, I mean?" He dropped his hands and stepped back. "I'm sorry. All I meant to say is if you need anything don't hesitate to call me. You still have my card?"

"Right by the telephone."

"Put it in your cell, also. Just in case."

"Will do."

He backed out of the small kitchen and threaded his way through the boxes in the living room to the front door. Lifting his jacket from the hook, he turned. "I'll let you know if something comes from the mannequin or the pictures—if the FBI lets me know and it's something we can share."

"That's a lot of ifs, but I'd appreciate it."

She stood at the door watching him saunter to his SUV with his long stride. The attraction between them was undeniable, but did his interest spring from the belief that she could help him with this case?

She slammed the door. It didn't matter anyway. In a few weeks, she'd be putting this case, this house, this town—and Sheriff Cooper Sloane in her rearview mirror.

ALMOST FOUR HOURS LATER, Kendall stepped into the hubbub of Sutter's Restaurant. Standing at the door inhaling the smell of charbroiled burgers, she let the chatter bubble over her.

This was exactly what she needed. After calling the cleaning crew and setting up an appointment, listening to her voice mail, talking to her best friend back home, checking in on a client who was having a minicrisis, and composing an online ad announcing the estate sale, she couldn't sit in that silent house one more minute. Aunt Cass hadn't even had a TV at the end. Her aunt had been quirky, but she'd tried her best to fill in for Kendall's missing-in-action parents, and Kendall had clung to her more than she had her own mother.

As her gaze traveled around the room, she had the distinct feeling people were avoiding her, looking away. Crud. Everyone must've already heard about the pictures buried on her property, and she'd become a walking black cloud. She didn't even have Melissa and Daryl to fall back on since they'd taken off for Seattle for a few days.

Kendall scooped in a big breath and smiled at the hostess. "Table for one, please."

"We have that one in the middle of the room or one by the kitchen."

"I'll take the one in the middle." She had no intention of hiding out by the kitchen, so she followed the hostess to the table set for four, squeezed between a family with two kids and a couple poring over a laptop together. Sutter's was known more for its food than its atmosphere anyway.

When her waitress showed up, Kendall ordered a beer and then snapped open the plastic menu.

"Mind if we join you?"

She edged down the menu and peered over the top at Coop, dressed in a pair of faded jeans and holding hands with an adorable girl with blond ringlets and big eyes as blue as her daddy's.

"Unless you want a quiet dinner by yourself." His mouth quirked into a smile. "But I think you picked the wrong place for that."

"You didn't want the table by the kitchen, either?" She smiled at Steffi. "Pull up a chair."

Coop settled his daughter in her seat, and then took the one across from Kendall. "Steffi, this is Ms. Rush."

Kendall waved. "Hi, Steffi. You can call me Kendall."

The little girl tilted her head to one side. "That's a funny name."

"Steffi, that's not polite," Coop said firmly.

Kendall widened her smile until it hurt. "Well, I like your name."

"It's really Stephanie but Steffi is easier. So everyone calls me Steffi."

"I like Stephanie, too. Are you in kindergarten?"

"Yes. My teacher is Mrs. Bryant and she has a long braid." She eyed Kendall's hair. "Longer than yours and we have a blue rug, but I told her I like pink better and we should have a pink rug instead of a blue rug, and then we read the book with the trains but I don't like the train book because Colby likes the train book and he likes the blue rug."

"Whew, I didn't realize kindergarten was filled with such drama."

Coop chuckled and rolled his eyes. "You had to ask."

Steffi opened her menu and pressed her lips together, ending the conversation.

Kendall let out a long breath between puckered lips when the waitress arrived at the table, tapping her pencil against her order pad. She drew up when she saw Coop and Steffi. "Oh, can I get you something to drink?"

"I'll have a beer." He pointed to Kendall's bottle. "What she's having. And my daughter will have a lemonade."

"Coffee, please." Steffi looked up from her menu and batted her lashes at the waitress.

The waitress raised her brows at Coop.

He shook his head. "Lemonade."

If Kendall had been expecting some shy, sad little girl missing her dead mother, Steffi had just blown that preconception out of the water. If she'd been expecting Coop's daughter to lavish affection on her dad's female friend, Steffi had blown that one out of the water, too.

"She's a pistol, Coop."

"Don't I know it?" He tapped his menu on the table. "Did you get everything done this afternoon?"

"Cleaning crew is coming tomorrow, and I advertised my estate sale. I even managed a telephone session with one of my patients."

"You do that?"

"If it's an emergency."

His eyes narrowed. "Was it an emergency?"

"A minor one." She took a sip of beer through the foam and studied his face. Why did he seem so interested in emergency telephone sessions when he'd given her the impression that he didn't put much stock in therapy? Maybe he could benefit from a little head shrinking.

He buried his un-shrunken head in the menu and gave Steffi some suggestions. "You don't always have to eat chicken nuggets."

"Have you had the hamburgers here yet, Steffi?"

"I like hamburgers, but no onions, no lettuce, no tomatoes, no pickles, no cheese."

"We get it, Steffi." Coop snapped his menu shut. "One burger, ketchup only."

"And onion rings." Kendall winked at Steffi. "We can share some onion rings."

"I don't like onions." Steffi wrinkled her nose.

"You'll like these. They're sort of like chicken nuggets but with onions inside instead of chicken."

Steffi screwed up her face and looked at the ceiling as if trying to picture onion nuggets.

The waitress returned with Coop's and Steffi's drinks and took their order. She jerked her thumb over her shoulder toward the hostess stand. "Do you want me to bring some crayons and a coloring book menu?"

Coop answered, "That would be great, thanks."

He clinked the neck of his bottle against her glass. "Cheers."

"Cheers." She took a sip of beer and dabbed her mouth with a napkin. "Have you heard anything yet from the FBI?"

"Had a conversation with Maxfield." He took the menu and crayons from the waitress, thanked her and put them in front of Steffi. "The parents were both relieved to see the pictures and horrified by the manner in which they were found."

"I can understand that." Kendall took a gulp of beer. "I suppose they haven't found any evidence on the boxes or pictures yet."

"Not yet, and there were no fingerprints or fibers on the mannequin."

Steffi looked up from her coloring. "What's a mannequin?"

Kendall glanced at Coop and put a finger to her lips. Kids tuned in to adult conversations more than the adults realized—at least that's what her clients told her.

Coop tweaked his daughter's nose. "A mannequin is like a big doll. Stores use them to show clothes."

"I know. They don't have any eyes or hair."

A little shiver crept across Kendall's flesh.

They dropped the conversation about mannequins and evidence and Polaroid photos showing kidnapped children. Kendall wasn't sure she could stomach her food if they hadn't.

After several more minutes of talking about the weather, the food at the party last night and the couple that seemed glued to their laptops, the waitress showed up with their food.

"Onion rings for the table, a pepper-jack burger, a house charbroil and a plain with ketchup." The waitress delivered their baskets of food with a flourish. "Anything else? Another round of beers?"

She and Coop both declined a second beer. Then Kendall shoved the basket of onion rings toward Steffi. "Do you want to try one?"

"I guess." Steffi hooked her finger around a ring and dropped it on her plate.

While they fussed with condiments and napkins, Kendall watched the interaction between Coop and his daughter. He seemed to have a good relationship with Steffi—joking and tender with just the right amount of parental sternness.

And for her part, Steffi had dropped the chilly attitude toward the woman who had butted in on the father-daughter dinner, not that the girl had actually warmed toward her. Kendall had always shied away from children, had absolutely refused to see any families or children in therapy. So, the slight chill from Steffi suited her just fine.

After she'd crunched through a few onion rings and had eaten half of her burger, Steffi tugged on her father's sleeve. "Look, Daddy. There's Genevieve. Can I go see her?"

"We don't want to disturb their meal." Coop twisted in his seat and waved at a family of four, the little girl bouncing in her seat in the booth and pointing at Steffi.

The woman cupped her hand and gestured Steffi over.

"Genevieve's mom says it's okay, but as soon as they get their food you need to come back here."

"Okay." Steffi was gone in a flash, squeezing into the booth next to her friend, whispering and giggling.

"Are the children worried about the kidnappings?"

Coop dragged an onion ring through a puddle of ketchup on his plate. "They're aware of the abductions, of course. One of the kids was a first-grader at their school. The other was homeschooled. We parents have warned them about stranger-danger and are much more diligent about keeping tabs on them. But you do know that both children were snatched from their homes, don't you?"

"Yes, just like the Timberline Trio."

He crunched the onion ring and swallowed. "So, the parents are definitely on edge. There was a little of that at the Rhodes party last night, although you might've missed it."

"Yeah, because everyone immediately stops talking about the kidnappings whenever I show up."

"They're just being sensitive."

"Do they have the same consideration for Wyatt?"

"Sort of, but it's different. He still lives here, and he's been doing some work at the police station so it's been kind of unavoidable for him."

"Has anyone started looking funny at Chuck Rawlings yet?"

"Oh, yeah."

"Has the FBI checked him out?"

"FBI checked him out just like the cops checked him out twenty-five years ago."

"Well, he is the only registered sex offender in Timberline."

"Not anymore."

"Really?" She dropped her burger and wiped her hands on the nearest napkin. "Did Evergreen Software bring a few more pervs to town?"

"In an indirect way. The *pervs* in question don't actually work for Evergreen, but the improved economy brought them here."

"That's just great. They all checked out?"

"Yep. Even old Chuck."

"I can't believe Chuck Rawlings had any alibis since he lives in that creepy, old cabin all by himself and rarely goes out. He was the same way when we were kids. We used to dare each other to play ding-dong ditch at his place."

"There's no evidence to connect Rawlings to the kidnappings—now or then." Coop did a quick slice of his finger across his throat, and then smiled. "Hey, Britt, I hope Steffi didn't disturb your family."

"Not at all. Genevieve wouldn't sit still until Steffi came over to the table." The petite blonde put her hands on Steffi's shoulders as her gaze kept shifting to Kendall. "And as soon as our food arrived, she told me she had to go back to your table."

"Good job, kiddo." Coop tugged on one of Steffi's curls. "Britt Fletcher, this is Kendall Rush. Kendall, Britt."

Kendall reached across the table and shook the other woman's hand. "Nice to meet you."

"You, too." Britt acted as if she wanted to say more. In fact, she acted as if she wouldn't mind conducting a thorough interrogation of her.

As if sensing Britt's curiosity, Coop dismissed her.

"Thanks for bringing her over. We'll let you get back to your family and your dinner."

Britt held up a hand, wiggled her fingers and returned to her table.

Instead of taking a seat, Steffi hung on the back of her chair. "Daddy, I'm tired. I wanna go home. I don't feel good."

"Really?" Coop's hand shot out to feel Steffi's forehead. "You're a little warm."

"My stomach hurts. I gotta leave *now*."

Coop half rose out of his chair, throwing an apologetic look her way.

"Go." Kendall flicked her hand in the air. "Get Steffi home."

He tucked three twenty-dollar bills beneath the saltshaker on the table. "Dinner's on me. I'll call you tomorrow."

She waved at Steffi whose lips were turned down in a pout. She either really did have a stomachache or she didn't like Daddy's new friend. And that's why Kendall never dated men with kids—one of many reasons.

The waitress returned to the table with the check. "Do you want to take any of this food with you?"

"No, thanks." She handed the waitress the sixty bucks, which was more than enough to cover the bill and the tip, and finished her beer.

Kendall weaved her way through the tables in the dining area and donned her jacket at the hostess stand. She pushed out of the restaurant, flipping up her hood against the drizzle.

The restaurant had been crowded when she'd arrived and all the good parking spots in the front had been taken, but she didn't mind the walk to her truck since it delayed her return to Aunt Cass's house.

She couldn't get the image out of her mind of some sick freak digging those holes by the side of the creek.

Pausing at a gift shop, she cupped her hand around her eyes and peered into the window. She grinned at the stuffed frog sitting on a shelf, its froggy legs dangling in space. Timberline had adopted the Pacific chorus frog as its town mascot years ago, and it appeared that even the high-tech vibe of Evergreen Software hadn't torpedoed the little frog's appeal.

She straightened up and walked past the corner of the shop. Two steps across the entrance of the alley, a whispering sound drew her attention. As she turned her head toward the sound, a strong arm grabbed her around the middle and yanked her into the alley.

Chapter Eight

Just as a scream gathered in her lungs, the vise around her middle dropped.

"Shh. Kendall, it's me, Wyatt."

She stumbled back, her fist pressed against her chest where her heart threatened to escape. "My God, Wyatt. Why did you do that? You scared me half to death."

"I'm sorry." In the shadows of the alley, Wyatt slumped against the wall of the building and covered his face. "I need help, Kendall. I don't want anyone to see me like this."

She licked her dry lips, her heart still pummeling her ribs. "What's wrong?"

He stuffed his hand into his jacket pocket and withdrew it slowly. "I found this on my porch today." He uncurled his fist to reveal a small dark object on the palm of his hand.

"I can't even see what it is." She took his wrist and pulled him closer to the light in the street. And then her stomach sank.

"A dinosaur." She picked up the plastic toy between two fingers as if it could come to life and nip a piece of flesh out of her hand.

"You know what it means, right?" The hand Wyatt still had outstretched trembled.

"The kidnapper left a plastic dinosaur when he took Harrison." Coop had told her not to mention the pink ribbon left at the scene of the first kidnapping or the dinosaur, but surely Wyatt knew anyway.

He snatched his hand back and covered his mouth with it. "What? No, no, no."

"Stop, Wyatt." She tugged on his sleeve.

He jerked away. "I never told you this, Kendall, but when my brother was kidnapped the guy who took him also took one of my dinosaurs from my collection."

Kendall crossed her arms. Just like he'd taken the pink ribbon from her hair. Did Wyatt not know before she'd told him that the present-day kidnapper had left a plastic dinosaur when he snatched Harrison?

The chill of the night had seeped into her bones. "Let's go inside Sutter's and get a beer."

"I can't go in there. Don't you see the way they look at us? It's almost like they blame us for this second wave of kidnappings. Heather Brice's family had it right by moving away from all this, away from the memories."

"I—I don't think they blame us." But Wyatt had nailed it. They were like two bad omens hovering over Timberline bringing bad news, reminding the residents of a past they'd rather forget, a past that interfered with their bright, shiny, tech future.

"I don't think you need to worry, Wyatt. You're a big guy. You can handle yourself, and you can handle a gun, too. Don't you still hunt?"

"Yeah, but it's not that, Kendall. It's not the physical." He drove the heels of his hands into his temples. "It's the memories. I miss my little brother every day. Don't you miss Kayla?"

"Of course, but we need to move on, Wyatt, or it'll drive us crazy." She felt for her phone in her pocket. "Give me your number. I'm going to look up a good therapist in the area. It can even be someone in the next town, so you don't run into anyone from Timberline if that's what you're worried about. You really need to get some help."

"I thought I could see you, Kendall. You're the only one who knows what I'm going through. I'll pay you."

"I can't see a friend as a client, Wyatt. It doesn't work that way. Besides, a therapist doesn't have to experience what you're experiencing to be able to help you." She tapped her phone. "Give me your number, so I can call you with a recommendation."

He closed his eyes and recited his number, which she entered into her phone. "You sure you don't want to go into Sutter's and have a beer? Relax a little?"

He grunted. "I already have one DUI on my record. I can't afford another."

"Okay, I don't want to encourage drinking and driving." She patted his arm. "Are you feeling better? You should tell Coop about the dinosaur even though it's probably just someone playing a trick. There's a lot of that going on."

"But nobody knew about the dinosaur he took from me. That wasn't released."

It had been the same with the pink ribbon, but that had been years ago. "Look, Wyatt, those old files have been passed around and seen by hundreds of pairs of eyes by now. Anything could've gotten out about the case."

If she could follow the advice she was dispensing so freely to Wyatt, she'd feel a lot better about going back to Aunt Cass's house by herself. But then therapists were great at dishing out advice to others that they didn't take themselves.

"I guess you're right, but I'll let Coop know. I've been on edge since this whole thing started."

"I think everyone has." She glanced at the sky. "I'm going to head home before the heavens open."

"Do you want me to walk you to your truck?"

She wanted to get away from Wyatt as far and as quickly as she could. "That's okay. Try to breathe and I'll get back to you with a therapist."

"Thanks, Kendall, and I'm sorry I scared you."

"I'm a little on edge, too, Wyatt."

Grasping the edge of the building, he leaned into the sidewalk and looked both ways. "Be careful, Kendall."

"I'm fine. The truck is close, and there are still lots of people out and about."

She raised her hand in a wave and started down the sidewalk, her boots clicking on the cement. She paused at a few more shop windows and at her second stop, became aware of a figure across the street paralleling her course down the sidewalk.

Flipping up the hood of her jacket, she jerked her head to the side, catching the man across the way illuminated by the light spilling from a candy shop. She sucked in a quick breath.

Chuck Rawlings hadn't changed much in twenty-five years. His long hair had turned silver, but he still carried himself hunched over as if guilty of something. He'd shoved a hand in his pocket and made a half turn toward the display of sweets in the window, but he'd been watching her and maybe even following her since Sutter's.

She lengthened her stride and bypassed the remaining shop windows to reach the truck. As she unlocked the door, she cranked her head over her shoulder. This time she met Chuck's eyes.

He'd stopped and turned toward the street, toward her. He nodded once and continued on his way, his silver ponytail swaying behind him.

Did he want a therapist, too? The man had been the one registered sex offender in town back in the day. As a kid, she'd had no idea what that meant. As an adult, she'd looked him up and discovered he'd had what he'd called consensual sex with a sixteen-year-old and a seventeen-year-old. Creepy, but hardly dangerous— unless you were a sixteen-year-old girl.

As she climbed behind the wheel it occurred to her that Wyatt hadn't even mentioned the pictures of the kidnapped children holding newspapers with the Timberline Trio headlines. He obviously hadn't heard about the discovery, and she was glad she hadn't been the one to tell him.

If a plastic dinosaur had sent him over the edge, what would those pictures have done to him?

She drove back to Aunt Cass's and left the truck in front of the house. Looking left and right, she unlocked the front door and scooted inside. She clicked the dead bolt into place and closed her eyes. First Wyatt and then Rawlings—must be something in the air tonight. She could use that security system Coop had suggested right now. His protectiveness gave her a warm and fuzzy feeling. Well, maybe not fuzzy but definitely warm.

She liked everything about the man. Too bad his daughter didn't like her, not that Kendall was the nurturing, maternal type with kids anyway.

She checked the windows and wandered into the kitchen to make some tea. As the water boiled on the kettle, she peered out the back door toward the creek. A few minutes later, her eyes ached trying to pick out shapes and movement in the forest.

The tea kettle screamed, and Kendall placed her palms against the cold glass of the window. *Please, God. Keep those children safe—even if You couldn't protect Kayla.*

THE FOLLOWING MORNING, Kendall showed the four-woman cleaning crew around the house. "Don't worry about the boxes. Clean around them, and maybe I can have you back out for a once-over with the vacuum and a mop once I get rid of this stuff."

"Do we have to go out there?" Annie, the group's spokeswoman, a Native American from the local Quileute tribe, jerked her head toward the patio.

"I'm going to hire a landscaping service to clean the patio and trim the bushes bordering it." Crossing her arms, Kendall drummed her fingers against her biceps. "Why?"

Annie placed one hand over her heart. "We heard about the pictures of the children buried by the creek."

"Yes, it was…unnerving. If it was the kidnapper

who planted those photos, he's not going to be back here, though. You'll be fine." Kendall added a bright smile to punctuate her words. If she kept telling everyone else how fine they'd be, maybe she could believe it of herself.

While the women hauled their cleaning supplies into the house, Kendall finished tagging the boxes—ones for the Salvation Army, ones to drag outside for the estate sale and ones for the online auction site. None to take home—she didn't need any more reminders of this damp, gloomy place once she'd escaped back to Phoenix. She had fond, warm memories of Aunt Cass. She didn't need her knick-knacks.

Someone tapped on the screen door.

Kendall scribbled on a box with black marker. "No need to stand on ceremony. You can come in and out as you please."

"That's mighty nice of you, ma'am."

She swiveled around at the sound of Coop's low, teasing voice that had started doing funny things to her insides.

"Oh, it's you!" She folded her legs beneath her and leaned against the stack of boxes. "I have some ladies helping me out with the rest of the cleaning today."

"I saw their van—Dreamweavers." He circled his finger in the air. "Is that what they're going to do? Weave dreams with their brooms and mops?"

"I hope so." Her gaze skimmed up and down his body, his long legs in a pair of worn jeans again, topped with a plaid flannel shirt with a blue T-shirt peeking out of the unbuttoned neck. "You're not on duty today? You're finally going to use that vacation time?"

"I'm not officially on duty, but as I mentioned be-fore—small department like this and I'm always on call." He tilted his cell phone back and forth. "I just came out to make sure you were okay and to see if you still wanted me to look into a security system for you."

"Absolutely." She met his gaze and a flash of un-derstanding passed between them. He wanted to check on her—and she wanted him here, wanted him close.

"There's a place in Port Angeles that carries a good supply."

"Oh, I was going to head up there in less than an hour, anyway." She stood up, brushing the seat of her leggings. "Give me the info and I can pick it up my-self."

"I want to make sure you get the right kind, and I can get a law enforcement discount." He scuffed the toe of his boot against the carpet. "You can ride with me. I'm not sure that old truck could make it."

A smile tugged at her lips. He didn't have to do any convincing. "That would be great. I just have a few er-rands to do, so I won't be there all day."

"Hell, we could make an event out of it and have lunch on the water."

"Perfect. Are you ready to go now?"

"I was on my way when I stopped here."

Grabbing handfuls of her baggy T-shirt, she stretched the hem down to her knees. "I just need to change into something warmer, and I'll be right with you."

She nudged one of the boxes with her toe. "Do you have room for a few of these boxes? I'm going to drop them off at a place that lists items on an online auction site, collects payment and ships them out."

"I have my truck. I'll load them up while you change." He waved. "Hey, there, Annie. I like the van."

"Hi, Coop." A broad smile claimed half of Annie's face. "My cousin Scarlett designed it for us."

"Tell her I said it looks great."

Kendall gave Annie a tight smile as she squeezed past her on the way to the back rooms. Did Coop's charm have the same effect on every female within a hundred-mile radius of him?

Not that she had any claim on the sexy sheriff—none at all.

As Coop loaded the last box in his truck bed, the front door of the house closed. He looked up, getting a great view of Kendall's backside as she bent forward to sweep up the freebie newspaper from the ground.

She'd swapped her black leggings for a pair of tight jeans that fit her almost as closely. She'd tucked those jeans into a pair of furry ankle boots, which she probably never wore in Phoenix.

Holding up the newspaper, she called out, "You want this?"

"I have about ten of them in a pile in my house."

She chucked the newspaper onto the porch and strode toward the door he was holding open for her. "Could you fit all the boxes in your truck?"

"With room to spare."

Planting one furry boot on the running board, she hoisted herself up. He grabbed her elbow to steady her.

"Whoa." She turned her face toward him, a laugh bubbling on her lips. "Why do guys like these trucks way up off the ground. I could get a nosebleed up here."

"It makes us feel superior."

"Are you sure you're not compensating for something?"

She winked and a surge of lust thundered through his veins. Her mouth softened and her eyes widened in a sure invitation to a kiss, or maybe her expression was a reaction to his. What did he look like when he wanted a woman so badly, he could already taste her?

He cleared his throat. "Now, what would we be compensating for?"

"I'll think about it, long and hard, and let you know later."

The woman was flirting with him. He slammed the door on her smirk and practically ran to the driver's side.

"Music or conversation?" His hand hovered at the power button for the radio.

"How about a little of both, as long as the music isn't too intrusive."

"I can do unintrusive. My truck came with that satellite radio, so you can find just about anything on there."

"This thing is all tricked out, isn't it?" She tapped the buttons, jumping from station to station, little blips and blurbs of music flashing by in a kaleidoscope of sound.

He gave her a sidelong glance as he pulled into the road. "Are you suggesting more overcompensation on my part?"

"I'm not going to say a word. I know when I've got it good." She pressed two fingers against her luscious lips. "I'd rather ride in comfort for the next hour or so, than in that rattle-trap truck of my aunt's."

They talked easily with a bantering, flirtatious tone that Coop hadn't used for a while, and that he hadn't expected from Kendall. But with each mile they traveled away from Timberline, Kendall's demeanor grew more and more relaxed. Her smile got brighter, her eyes grew clearer and the stiff way she'd held herself eased.

As she laughed, teased and sang snatches of songs from the radio, she spun a web around him with her charm and natural sexiness.

The exit for Port Angeles appeared way too quickly. He could've driven all the way to Alaska in her company.

He rolled his shoulders. "How do you want to do this? I can drop you off and then go look at the security systems myself, and then pick you up or we can meet at a restaurant by the water for lunch."

"That sounds like a plan." She flipped down the visor and rolled some lipstick across her mouth. "I don't want to bore you with the auction stuff, and my other errand is confidential."

He whistled. "Ooh, confidential."

"It's really not that exciting." She smacked her lips together and smacked the visor back up with the palm of her hand. "I have your number. I'll call when I'm ready. If I'm done earlier than you, I can probably get a bus down to the water."

"Deal." He tipped his chin toward the windshield. "Where am I going now?"

Swiping her index finger across her phone's display, she said, "Let me check the address."

She tapped the screen a few more times and a robotic, female voice started reciting directions from the cell phone.

He followed her orders until the truck was idling in front of a row of one-story shops. "Do you see it?"

"It's the business in the middle with the box on the sign."

"The security place is a few miles away. Do you have any preferences before I buy your system?"

"You're the expert. Just make sure you find me something that's going to stop people from creeping around my property, digging graves." She hopped from the truck.

He met her at the truck bed and unloaded the boxes. "Open the door for me, and I'll carry them in."

She held open the door of the shop, and he stacked the boxes inside.

Putting his lips close to her ear just to breathe in her scent, he whispered. "Don't let them take advantage of you."

He drove the two miles with his mind in a jumble. He needed to back away from Kendall Rush even though every male part of his body urged him forward.

She'd made it clear she had no intention of sticking around Timberline. At least that's one thing Kendall and Steffi had in common—they both hated the Pacific Northwest, or at least this particular town in the Pacific Northwest.

If Kendall planned to hightail it out of here as soon as she settled her aunt's affairs and listed the house, they'd only have time for a superficial quickie—not that he had anything against superficial quickies, especially with a woman like Kendall, but it would be a bad move on his part.

Despite her shell, Kendall had soft, squishy insides. Her dark brown eyes always held a tinge of sadness. The twin who was no longer a twin.

He couldn't take advantage of a woman's vulnerability—not again.

He threw the truck into Park and pushed through the two glass doors of the security shop.

"Can I help you?"

The clerk behind the counter pounced on the only customer in the store.

Coop approached the glass case and dragged his finger across the top of a few of them until he found the security items. "I need to put together a system for a house—motion-sensor lights, cameras, the works."

"We can do that." The clerk launched into an explanation of all the high-tech gadgets and the must-haves.

Coop got into the spirit so much so that the guy must've thought he wanted to protect Fort Knox.

But he wanted to protect something much more precious than gold—he wanted to protect Kendall Rush.

JESSA PATTED THE last box. "I'll send you an email verifying all your prices on the items, and if I see anything of real value I'll recommend a higher price. You know the auction site charges a percentage for listing on top of the percentage I charge for handling the listing?"

"Yeah, I know that. Totally worth it." Kendall picked up a pair of gold lamé boots. "Really?"

"Supposedly they belonged to Elvis." Jessa shrugged.

Kendall snorted. "Right. I'll leave it all in your capable hands, Jessa. I'll be in Timberline for another week or two if you need me to come back."

"I've got all your contact info." She flicked her finger against the computer monitor.

Kendall held her phone up to her face and tapped it for the address of Dr. Jules Shipman. "Can you tell me how far I am from the five-hundred block of Marine Avenue?"

"Marine runs east-west, and I think the five hundreds are east of here." Jessa pointed a finger out the window. "That's left if you keep going up the street."

"Can I walk?"

"It's about a mile, but I can give you a lift. I was just about to go out to the office supply store."

"I don't want to put you to any trouble."

Jessa cupped her hand around her mouth. "Tony, I'm heading out. Can you watch things up here?"

"Got it, babe. Don't forget the shipping tape. We're down to two."

She called back. "On my list."

Jessa grabbed a set of keys from a hook behind her desk, and Kendall followed her out the front door.

She scooted into the passenger seat of Jessa's car, which was emblazoned with ads for her business.

"What's the address?" Jessa pulled away from the curb without even checking her mirrors, and Kendall's fingers curled around the edge of the seat.

"It's 538 Marine."

"Yeah, that's definitely left." Jessa's little car covered the mile faster than Kendall thought possible and when she screeched to a stop in front of a two-story office building, Kendall shot out of the car. "Thanks, Jessa. I'll be in touch about the items."

Jessa waved and squealed away from the curb.

Shaking her head, Kendall walked under the overhang of the building and headed toward the directory behind a glass case on the stucco wall. She'd confirmed Jules's office number on the phone this morning but wanted to verify first.

Murmuring the number, she turned toward the first office—number too high. The one she was looking for must be the office in the front, the door she'd passed on her way to the directory.

When she reached the office of Dr. Jules Shipman, her cell phone buzzed. "Hi, Coop. Are you done already?"

"Almost, give me about ten minutes."

"I'll be about twenty more minutes, so go ahead and find a place for lunch and I'll meet you there."

"I'll look up something on my phone, and I'll swing by and pick you up. I don't mind waiting."

Her gaze wandered to the nameplate on the wall next to the door. There were lots of offices in this building. Coop didn't have to know she was visiting a therapist for Wyatt.

"Okay. I'll try to hurry up." She gave him the address of the building next door and ended the call.

She pocketed her phone and hunched forward, pressing her ear against the office door. That didn't tell her a thing. Turning the handle slowly, she eased open the door, peeking into the empty waiting room.

She let out a breath. Before she could take another

step into the room, a dark-haired woman burst from the door on the other side.

"Kendall Rush?"

Kendall let the door swing shut behind her. "Yes, nice to meet you, Dr. Shipman."

The woman tilted her head to one side, and a lock of hair slipped from her messy bun. "You can call me Jules, and you know I'm not a psychiatrist."

"But you're a Ph.D."

"Yeah, but that doctor stuff sounds so pretentious. Do you have your Ph.D.?"

"Nope, just my master's in clinical psych."

"I wish I could tell you the doctorate commands more money, but it doesn't, not in private practice, anyway."

"I had heard that. Thanks for seeing me on such short notice."

"No problem." She swiveled her wrist inward. "My next client's not due for another twenty-five minutes."

"I won't take up too much of your time. As I mentioned on the phone, my friend is having some difficulties dealing with the kidnappings in Timberline because his brother was one of the Timberline Trio. Are you familiar with the case?"

"I didn't grow up here, so I hadn't heard about the case until these recent kidnappings. Horrible. I can't imagine the pain this man feels right now."

Kendall gave a curt nod with no intention of revealing her own connection to the case. "Last night he pleaded with me to help him, but I explained that therapy with me wouldn't work."

"I'd be happy to see him. I'm not quite at full capacity now, and I see a lot of clients from the surrounding smaller towns like Timberline. Do you want to ask me any questions?"

"Just a few." Kendall proceeded to ask Jules about her methods and her practice, and they even commiserated about the pitfalls of the profession.

At the end of their discussion, Kendall had a good feeling about Jules.

"I think you'd be great for Wyatt. Can I have your card? In fact, I'll take a couple."

"They're in my office." She jerked her thumb over her shoulder.

Kendall followed her into the inner sanctum, a soothing environment with low lights, comfy chairs, plants and scenic art on the walls—looked exactly like her own office.

Jules plucked several cards from the holder on her desk. "Here you go. Have Wyatt call me anytime he's ready."

"I'd better make way for your next client." Kendall thrust out her hand. "Thanks so much for meeting with me."

"Absolutely." Jules walked her into the outer office. "I actually have a client who moved to Phoenix recently. I might be able to return the favor and give you a referral."

Kendall slipped out the front door and immediately saw Coop's truck idling at the curb. Damn. She should've given him an address half a block down so he wouldn't see her coming out of Dr. Shipman's office, even though there was no way he could read the nameplate from the street. Hopefully, he'd know not to ask questions.

Tugging her jacket closed, she practically skipped toward the truck. She couldn't wait to sit down with Coop and have lunch. She grabbed the door handle and yanked.

"Sorry to keep you waiting…" Her voice trailed off as she took in Coop's profile, hard as a block of ice and just as cold.

Then he turned toward her and she flinched at the pain in his eyes.

"What kind of sick game are you playing, Kendall?"

Her foot slipped from the running board and her knee banged against the passenger seat. "Wh-what?"

He leveled a finger at her. "Are you going to deny you were in Jules Shipman's office? Don't even try. I saw you coming out of there."

"I don't understand. What's going on?"

"Did you have your little confidential conversation with Dr. Shipman? Did she tell you she killed my wife?"

Chapter Nine

Kendall jerked back. Whatever she'd expected to come out of Coop's mouth—that wasn't it.

"Killed your wife? What are you talking about? You know Jules Shipman?"

His brows shot up. "Oh, that's how it's gonna be?"

She closed her eyes, took a deep breath and hoisted herself into the truck. They couldn't continue this crazy conversation on the sidewalk. Jules's next client might hear them.

"What is going on, Coop? You need to back up several steps here." She swept her hands across her face as if trying to get a fresh start. "Dr. Shipman didn't mention your wife. I didn't realize you and your wife knew Jules. I saw her on…business."

He peeled one hand from the steering wheel, where he'd been squeezing it with a white-knuckle grip, and covered his mouth. He stared out the window for several seconds. "Are you telling me the truth?"

Okay, he'd almost regained his senses.

"I'm telling you the truth. I never met Dr. Shipman before today. I looked her up, along with a couple of other therapists in town, and she happened to be the only one who was free to talk to me this morning." She held up two fingers. "I swear."

"God, I feel so stupid." He leaned his forehead against the steering wheel. "I'm sorry I went off on you."

She touched his shoulder. "Do you want to tell me about it? If there's something I should know about Dr. Shipman..."

The muscles across his back tensed. "She's a quack."

"What happened with Dr. Shipman, Coop?"

Lifting his bowed head, he rolled his shoulders and put the truck in motion. "We have a reservation at the Pelican's Nest."

Kendall snapped her seat belt and sank against the seat. That lunch she'd been looking forward to had just lost its appeal. The tension in the truck was about as thick as a Washington Peninsula cloud cover, and she didn't dare open her mouth in case it set Coop off again.

He drove down to the port in silence and paid for parking in a public lot. The hostess showed them to their table, one with a beautiful view, but Kendall barely noticed it.

She sat across from Coop and ordered a glass of white wine. She could use about five of them.

Reaching across the table, he took her hand. "I'm sorry, Kendall."

"Look, I don't know what just happened back there, but can we wipe the slate clean and just enjoy our lunch before leaving? Unless you want to leave right now."

A spasm of pain crossed his face. "My wife, Alana, committed suicide."

Her hand twitched beneath his. "I'm so sorry."

"She took a bunch of pills while in the bathtub, although I guess it doesn't matter how she did it."

She ran the pad of her thumb along the knuckles of his hand. Now she understood. Jules had been seeing Alana, and now he blamed the therapist for Alana's death. That was such a common reaction even if it wasn't based in reality.

"Depression?"

"When Alana finally admitted it to me, told me how much she was suffering, I tried to get her help. I tried, but it ended in disaster. Dr. Jules Shipman was a disaster."

Kendall bit her lip, literally and figuratively. If Coop had been putting his faith in Jules to rescue his wife, he was destined for disappointment. Therapists weren't miracle workers.

The waitress arrived, and Coop snatched his hand back as she delivered their drinks and took their orders.

He poured his mineral water into the glass and studied the bubbles for a few seconds. "You're going to defend her, Dr. Shipman, aren't you?"

"I don't know what went on in their sessions, and neither do you, but psychotherapy can only do so much for a depressed patient. Pharmaceuticals play a bigger role in managing depression and suicidal thoughts."

"Have you ever lost a patient...like that?"

She blinked. "Two."

"Did the families blame you?" He cupped her wineglass in his hand and took a sip.

"One did, one didn't. It's not easy for anyone." She shoved the wineglass back toward him. "Have another."

"When I saw you coming out of her office—" he tugged on his earlobe "—I thought... I don't know what I thought."

"That I was spying on you? Gathering intel on you for some nefarious purpose?" She traced her finger around the base of her glass. "Why didn't you tell me your wife committed suicide? Timberline is a small town. You know I would've found out sooner or later, and what difference would it make? It's something I would rather hear from you."

"I knew you'd find out. I just didn't want to be the one to admit my failure."

His admission didn't surprise her. Relatives, especially spouses, always felt the guilt, and that's why they blamed the mental health professionals.

Crossing his arms over his chest, he leaned back in his chair. "You're not going to jump in and tell me it wasn't my fault? I don't have any reason to feel guilty?"

"No."

A muscle in his jaw ticked and he reached for the wine again. "Once I discovered the way she was feeling, I did everything in my power to help her."

"I believe you."

"Including sending her to see Dr. Shipman." His nostrils flared as he shifted the blame from himself to Jules.

"It feels good to blame someone besides yourself, doesn't it?"

"You think I'm blaming Dr. Shipman because I really blame myself, don't you?"

"You wouldn't be the first."

The waitress approached their table, a plate in each

hand. "Fish and chips and the salmon fettucine. Can I get you anything else?"

Coop held up a finger. "Vinegar, please."

"And another glass of chardonnay." Kendall held up her half-empty glass.

When the waitress walked away, Coop's lips twisted. "I promise I won't steal any more of your wine. Therapy session over."

"Just because we talk about more than the weather, doesn't mean I'm playing therapist. I'm playing friend and I care what happens to you and your daughter." She picked up her fork. "I'm just happy you don't believe I was skulking around behind your back."

"What *were* you doing at her office?"

Kendall ran the tip of her finger along the seam of her lips. "Confidential, remember? We don't kiss and tell."

"Right. Sorry." He bit into a piece of fish with a crunch. "Time to change the subject. I got a good security system for you. If there's time this afternoon, I'll start installing it at the house. I'm back at work tomorrow."

"I can get Lester Jenkins to install it. He's handy with that sort of thing."

"Or I can start on it and Lester can finish it off."

"What time is Steffi done with school? Don't you need to pick her up?"

"She goes home with Genevieve's mom—you met her last night at Sutter's. I never know from week to week what days I'm taking off, so it's just easier and more consistent for her to go to her friend's house."

He pointed a French fry at her plate. "Are you eating or talking?"

"Eating." She shoved her fork into the pasta and twirled.

The lunch hadn't gotten off to the best start, but as they both started to relax the food tasted better, the view looked more spectacular and she'd become much more witty.

Maybe that last part had to do with the wine buzzing through her veins. She even had Coop laughing about the gold lamé Elvis boots...and she liked to hear Coop laugh.

They finished lunch on a high note, and she insisted on paying since he'd gotten dinner the night before and he wouldn't take her money for the security system.

The drive back to Timberline proved to be even more relaxing, especially with a glass and a half of wine coursing through her system. She must've dozed off because when the truck hit a bump in the road and her eyelids flew open, they were passing the Quileute Indian Reservation.

She yawned and skimmed her tongue across her teeth. "I wonder if Annie and her crew are done with the house yet."

"You'd already cleaned half of it. I'm sure they are."

Kendall waved to a little girl by the side of the road selling trinkets with her mother. "You know, Annie didn't want to do any cleaning outside."

"They don't do outdoor work. If you need someone, I can find someone for you."

"It wasn't just the work." She trailed her finger down the inside of the window, following a drop of moisture on the outside. "She was afraid to go out there because of the crosses by the creek."

"I'm sure it's gonna affect a lot of people that way. The area is cordoned off, anyway."

"I know I sound like Rebecca, but I hope it doesn't affect the sale of the house. It already has one strike against it because of the crime committed there twenty-five years ago."

"I'm sure outsiders aren't going to care one way or the other. They'll probably come in and tear the whole place down."

"I hope they do."

He gave her a quick look, and then shifted his gaze back to the highway. "You don't have any happy memories of Timberline? Is that why you left and never came back?"

"I have some happy memories, but that one tragedy overshadows everything. It didn't stop with Kayla's kidnapping. My parents never had the most stable marriage to begin with, and losing Kayla put even more stress on them. My parents divorced and my mom slipped into a kind of madness. She's in a rest home in Florida now, and Dad passed away earlier than he should have. Aunt Cass never wanted kids, but she did her best in her own way."

"I'm sorry. Some families never do recover."

"So, I could never be truly happy here. Besides, I hate all the rain."

He chewed on his bottom lip and heaved a sigh. "Steffi hates the rain, too. Do you think…"

"What?"

"After trashing your profession, I feel like a hypocrite asking for your advice."

"Ask away. I don't think you're a hypocrite." He was a man who still blamed himself for his wife's suicide and found some relief in turning his wrath on her therapist.

"Steffi was just a baby when Alana killed herself, nineteen months old to be exact."

Kendall's nose stung with tears. How was Steffi going to feel when she got older and understood what her mother had done?

"That's sad." She sniffled.

"It was raining that day—hard. You know how it gets sometimes? That unrelenting rain that pours from the clouds."

"I remember it well."

"I was working and Alana had dropped Steffi off with a babysitter and never came back to get her. I was overwhelmed when I came home and found Alana in the tub. The babysitter offered to keep Steffi with her for the night." He smacked the steering wheel with the heel of his hand. "I never should've allowed that."

"Wait." She tapped her fingers lightly on his corded forearm. "You can't blame yourself for that. You did the right thing. Police, ambulance, her mother's body. Do you really think Steffi would've felt any sense of security or normalcy about all that?"

"So, her mother dropped her off and Steffi never saw her again, and it rained and rained that day and into the night like it would never stop." His arm tensed beneath her touch. "I think that's why Steffi hates the rain so much. Is that crazy? She was only nineteen months old."

"That's not crazy at all. You're probably right."

He blew out a breath as he made the turn toward Aunt Cass's house. "I'm really sorry. I thought this would be a nice day-trip to Port Angeles to get your mind off of everything going on here, and I brought down the whole mood."

"Life rarely follows a plan."

"Ain't that the truth? But I should've kept my mouth shut when I saw you coming out of Dr. Shipman's office. I snapped. If I'd taken a couple of deep breaths, I'd have realized you had no reason to be checking me out."

She had every reason to check him out—just not the way he meant.

"Sometimes our minds jump to the fastest conclusion, even if it's not the most logical."

He pointed to the Dreamweavers van in the drive. "Looks like Annie and her crew are still here."

"They must be doing a thorough job."

"I'm going to start installing your system before I pick up Steffi, unless you're anxious to get rid of me."

"You don't always have to be the smiling, helpful sheriff, Coop. You're allowed to have emotions."

"How would having a sheriff running around falling apart instill confidence? And you're one to talk. You're kind of tightly wound yourself." He parked his truck behind hers.

"Therapists can't run around falling apart, either."

Turning, he traced a finger along her jaw. "You're

not my therapist so any time you need to let go, I'll be there."

Her lashes fluttered, and she almost let go right then and there, confessing her overwhelming attraction to him, even though he hated therapists and his daughter was lukewarm about her.

She coughed. "I'll take you up on that offer...for as long as I'm in Timberline."

"That's what I meant." He threw open the door of the truck. "I'm going to get started."

She slid from the truck and peeked into the house. The antiseptic smell that greeted her made her nose twitch.

Annie poked her head around the entrance to the kitchen. "We're almost done. See anything you'd like us to do before we leave?"

"It smells so clean." Kendall took a deep breath. "I'm sure it's fine."

"Then we'll start packing up our stuff."

Kendall shed her jacket and hung it up in the closet. "Annie, do you know any landscapers who could use a one-time job? Mostly cleaning up and clearing out. I don't want to do anything too fancy since the new owners might do a teardown."

"Quileute?" Annie leaned a mop and two brooms against a stack of boxes in the corner. "Are you looking for someone from the rez?"

"Sure."

Annie shook her head, and then gave one of her workers a little shove. "Take these out to the van, Lucy."

Lucy took her time collecting the cleaning supplies, her gaze darting between Annie and Kendall.

When she banged through the screen door, Annie sighed. "Kendall, no Quileute is ever going to work on this land."

Kendall wedged her hands on her hips. "Because of the buried photos? Is it fear...or something else?"

"It's not just the recent discovery."

"You mean my sister's disappearance." She tapped the toe of her boot, trying to appear nonchalant. "You're here, and Lucy and the others."

"I had to use threats to get them to come." She raised her palms to the ceiling. "And I'm only half joking."

"You're not...superstitious?"

"Is that what you'd call it? Would you call yourself superstitious?"

"No."

"And yet you left this place as soon as you could and never returned, and now that Cass has passed on you can't wait to dump her belongings and get out of town."

"You got me." She smacked her palm against her chest. "What would you call it, then? An aura?"

She snorted. "I call it a job, but you could ask my cousin Scarlett. She's the shaman."

"I remember that. Maybe I will."

"I think you'll be gone before she comes back. She's also a famous artist now and she's down in San Francisco for a show of her work."

"That's great." A shadow passed across the window, and Kendall lifted the curtain to watch Coop lean a ladder against her house. "You don't know anyone who shares your skepticism of the bad aura and needs a few days' work?"

"Most landscapers are pretty busy these days work-

ing for the Evergreen families, but you might check
with Gary Binder. He's not Quileute, but he's been
doing odd jobs since he got out of prison."

"Prison?"

"Drugs—using, selling, manufacturing."

"Doesn't surprise me." She remembered Gary as a
morose, moody young man, but he had to be over forty
now. "I think I'll pass."

"He's clean and sober, could use the work."

"Is he any good?"

"For what you want? He'll do, and the man needs a
break. Everyone needs a break now and then." Annie
dipped and grabbed the handle of the plastic bucket at
her feet. "Let me know if you want us to come back
when you get all the furniture and boxes out of here."

"Will do." Kendall dug into her purse for her wallet and pulled out the cash she'd gotten from the ATM
earlier that morning. "Thanks a lot, Annie."

Kendall stood on the porch and waved to the other
women. "Thanks, ladies."

When they drove off in the van painted by a famous
artist, Kendall crossed her arms and leaned against
a white post on the porch. "Did you realize that the
Quileute think my house is haunted?"

"Makes sense." He pounded a nail into an eave. "I
don't claim to be any expert on the Quileute since I
haven't been here that long, but some of the tribe members do seem to have a heightened sensitivity to other-
worldly phenomena."

"Is that what you'd call it?"

"I suppose so." He strung a wire between two nails.
"I'm setting up the infrastructure for the security sys-

tem. I can finish it up tomorrow. I can probably get it done faster than Lester."

"That would be great." She scuffed some dirt from her porch with the toe of her boot. "Big plans tonight?"

"As a matter of fact, yes. It's back-to-school night and the principal asked me to give a presentation to the parents about safety."

"That was unheard of in this town until the Timberline Trio went missing. Even a few years after the kidnappings, when the shock had subsided, Timberline had gone back to the good old days. Even I was allowed free reign in the woods and on my bike with the other kids. People slowly started leaving their doors unlocked again."

"Yep. That's the town we moved to when Alana was pregnant with Steffi, and we had almost five solid years of that security." He climbed down from the ladder. "I'm going to return this to the side of the house and put the rest of the system pieces inside. Is that okay?"

"What's a few more boxes in the living room?"

"Are you going to be okay here tonight?"

"Absolutely. I still have my work cut out for me."

Coop folded the aluminum ladder and hitched it beneath one arm. While he carried it around the side of the house, Kendall scooped up the various boxes and pieces of equipment for her security system and carried them inside.

She met Coop at the door. "Do you have everything?"

"Just wish I'd had more time to get the system up and running." He scratched his stubble. "Maybe you can go visit Melissa and Daryl."

"They're on a romantic getaway in Seattle." She tucked her hair behind one ear and gave him a half-hearted smile. "I'll be fine. I'm going to take a look around town at some of the new shops that have gone in since the last time I visited Aunt Cass, which was before Evergreen moved here."

Reaching forward, he cupped her face with one hand. "Be careful, Kendall. Someone has decided to play some sick game with you."

"Not just me."

"What?" He dropped his hand.

She'd just torpedoed any moment they could've had. Maybe her instincts were kicking in to protect her from another sort of danger.

"Wyatt. Someone left a plastic dinosaur for Wyatt. I told him to mention it to you."

"Why didn't he?" His brows collided over his nose. "He's been working at the station. You'd think he would've told me if he told you."

"I'm not sure. I told him you'd want to know."

"Why would he want to keep it from me?"

"You'll have to ask him, but don't say you heard anything from me."

"That might not be possible because I'm going to ask him about it and I'm going to ask him to turn that dinosaur over, although there's probably not much hope of getting any prints now." He smacked the doorjamb. "Take care and call me if you need anything."

With the Dreamweavers and Coop gone, that old silence settled on the house again. What she wouldn't give for a fifty-six-inch flat screen and a hefty dose of reality TV right now.

She had to replace the emptiness with something, so she booted up her laptop and started playing her music library. Humming to the music in the background, she created some signs for the estate sale, exchanged a few emails with Jessa regarding the auction price of her aunt's items and checked her emails and voice mails.

No emergencies from any of her clients, and thank God she didn't have any with suicidal ideation at the moment. Had Coop expected Dr. Shipman to work miracles with his wife? No wonder he was leery of her profession.

She'd almost forgotten the reason she'd visited Dr. Shipman. She reached for her phone and tapped in Wyatt's number. It went straight to voice mail.

"Hi, Wyatt. It's Kendall. I found a therapist for you in Port Angeles. I think she'll be good for you. Her name is Dr. Shipman. I'll give you her number and you can call her when you're comfortable."

She reached into her purse hanging on the back of the chair and pulled out one of Dr. Shipman's cards. She recited the number for Wyatt, and then ended the call.

Stretching her arms over her head, she yawned. She'd better get her second wind because she had no intention of eating alone in this house tonight.

Her heart jumped when the screen at the front creaked open and someone pounded on the front door.

With her phone in one hand, she crept toward the front. Her aunt didn't even have a peephole in the door. She placed a hand on the doorknob and leaned forward. "Who is it?"

"It's Gary Binder, ma'am. Annie Foster said you needed some help clearing the property out here."

She leaned her forehead against the door. Darn that Annie. Couldn't she let her make her own decisions? If she didn't open the door, he'd think she was holding his prison term against him. If she did, he could force his way in here.

And do what? Make her take drugs?

She pulled in a deep breath and swung open the door. She put her poker face into action as she stared into the faded blue eyes of Gary Binder. A long scar from the corner of his eye to just beneath his earlobe emphasized the other deep lines on his face, and he wasn't trying to hide anything as he wore his graying hair cropped close to his head. He was a forty-five-year-old man inhabiting a sixty-five-year-old body.

"Hi, Gary. News spreads fast. I just told Annie about a few hours ago I was looking for someone." Her gaze wandered to the darkening sky behind him. He couldn't wait until morning?

"Annie knows I'm always looking." He ran a hand over the bristle on his head. "I ain't gonna lie to you, ma'am. I've been in and out of the joint and in and outta rehab but I'm clean and sober now and just lookin' to pick up some work here and there."

"I get it." She pointed past his shoulder. "I need the brush cut back here in the front and some general cleanup in the back—just down to the edge of the woods. Do you think you're up to it?"

He spread his lips into a gap-toothed smile. "I may look like hell, ma'am, but I'm strong and wiry. I can do this work, but I don't have a lot of tools of my own."

"I'm sure my aunt Cass has something in the shed by the side of the house."

Gary's face brightened up, making him look ten years younger.

"And I'll tell you what. When you're done with the job, you can keep whatever tools you find in there."

"Instead of pay? I guess I can do that."

"No, no. I'll pay you. I have to clear out all that stuff anyway. You can have it."

"Thank you, ma'am. Just tell me what needs to get done and I'll do it."

"It's a little late, Gary. Can you come back tomorrow? Maybe around ten o'clock…in the morning."

"Sure thing. I just wanted to get a jump on the job in case you were lookin' to hire someone else. Those Quileute? They ain't gonna work here anyway."

"Yeah, Annie told me that." She rubbed her arms as a rash of goose bumps raced across them. "So, tomorrow at ten?"

"Yes, ma'am."

She watched him walk down the drive with a peculiar jerky stride and yank a bicycle off the ground by its handlebars.

When she shut the door, she let out a breath. He wasn't so bad. He looked pretty rough, but she hadn't seen any signs that he was using.

Before any more nocturnal visitors could make their way to her front door, she slipped on her boots, grabbed a jacket and headed out for dinner.

The rain had stopped for the day, but Kendall pulled up her hood anyway as she scuffed through the leaves toward the truck. The first thing Gary could do was rake up all the leaves and needles on the drive. She planned to put most of Aunt Cass's stuff out here for the estate sale so she didn't have people traipsing through the house. The weatherman hadn't forecast any rain for the weekend.

She grabbed the handle of the truck and yanked open the door. It seemed to be creaking even louder than it had been yesterday.

A piece of paper fluttered beneath the windshield wiper. She slid out of the truck and plucked it free.

Squinting, she held the paper toward the light spilling from the truck. The slick paper had housing info printed on it—looked like one of Rebecca's open house flyers—but it was just a piece, a half sheet of paper.

She turned it over and drew in a sharp, cold breath.

Someone had left her a note in a spidery black scrawl. She clambered back inside the truck and punched on the dome light with her knuckle.

She read the note aloud. "Kendall, meet me at my house later. I know something about the pink ribbon."

Chuck Rawlings had printed his name in block letters at the end of the note.

Her gaze shifted to her rearview mirror. When had Chuck left this note on her truck?

She smoothed her thumb across the shiny paper—dry. It had to have been after they had come home because she would've noticed it on the way into the house. Why hadn't Chuck just come to her door?

Why hadn't he talked to her last night when he'd obviously been following her down the sidewalk?

The hand holding the note trembled and she dropped the paper onto the passenger seat. Was this some kind of trick to lure her to his cabin? Not that she was young and fresh enough to catch his perverted interest. She was no sixteen-year-old girl to fear his advances.

From the looks of his gaunt appearance last night, she could probably take him down with a few of the moves she'd learned in her self-defense class...unless he had a weapon.

She picked up the note again. If he knew something about the pink ribbon, maybe he knew something about the kidnapper even if he didn't realize it.

Turning the key in the ignition, she glanced at the clock on the dashboard. Coop was still at the open house. Maybe Rawlings did have some information and didn't want to bring attention to himself by calling Coop or, worse, the FBI.

If Rawlings could tell her something about the ribbon, she could help Coop. Then that FBI agent would have to listen to him.

She read the note again. Later? What did he mean by "later"? She peered at the dark sky with a sliver of moon peeking out from behind a cloud. Looked later to her.

It took her ten minutes to drive to Rawlings's cabin. His truck was parked by the side of the property, under a spotlight. Another spotlight illuminated a circle that encompassed his front porch and half of his driveway. Rawlings had his own security system.

For some reason, she closed the door of the truck just enough to kill the interior lights but she didn't slam it shut. She didn't want to alert him to her presence—not that she expected to catch him performing a human sacrifice or anything—she just preferred having the element of surprise.

She crept up to Chuck's house and stalled when the first step to his porch creaked beneath her foot. She straightened her backbone and took the next two steps with purpose. Chuck had asked her here, and she had nothing to fear from him.

Not seeing a doorbell, she rapped her knuckles against the frame of the screen door. She took a step back and laced her hands in front of her, muscles coiled for action.

In her head, she rehearsed the lines she'd say to him. She'd start out friendly, grateful for the info, but he'd better not be toying with her because she planned to get to the bottom of this and she had every intention of relating their conversation to Coop.

But Chuck had to open the door first.

She tugged on the handle of the screen door, and knocked on the heavy wood of the front door. As soon as her knuckles hit the wood, the door inched open.

Leaning toward the crack in the door, she called out. "Mr. Rawlings? Chuck?"

A soft whine answered her, and a furry, gray paw emerged from the bottom of the gap.

"Hey, little guy." She crouched and touched her finger to his velvety, black nose. "Where's your owner?"

The dog mewled and scrabbled for freedom, his claws clicking against the wood.

Kendall tried again. "Mr. Rawlings? Are you there? It's Kendall Rush. I got your note."

This time the dog barked, a high-pitched sound that ended on a little growl.

Pulling her bottom lip between her teeth, Kendall rose. Chuck Rawlings was not a young man and from the looks of him last night, not a particularly healthy one. Maybe the excitement over revealing what he knew about the pink ribbon had gotten the best of him. As far as she knew, he had no relatives in the area to check up on him.

She placed one hand against the door and shuffled her feet close to the opening to keep the dog from bolting. She pushed the door open, moving into the open space to block the dog. "Mr. Rawlings? Are you okay?"

She let the screen door bang behind her, while keeping the front door open.

A fire dying in the grate warmed the room, and a lamp on an end table cast a circular yellow glow that encompassed a pair of slippers dropped haphazardly by the side of the sofa. Their frayed ends indicated that they'd been nibbled on by the little mutt at her feet.

She swallowed hard. Where was Rawlings? Lying in wait in his bedroom or behind the door with an ax?

The little dog pranced around her ankles, and pawed at her jeans. Would an ax murderer have a little precious like this?

Dipping down, she chucked the pooch under the chin. "Did you chew your master's slippers, you naughty pup? And where is your master?"

He licked her fingers and jumped up again, dragging his paws down her shin. The dog's presence calmed her jumpy nerves, and he could be her protection in case Rawlings did come at her.

"You little rascal. Do you want to be my body-guard?" She cupped her arm beneath his body to swoop him up and noticed several spots he'd left on her jeans. She brushed at the smudges, drawing her brows over her nose at the moist feel of the stain.

She turned her hand over, studying the dark smear on her fingers. She released the squirming mutt and staggered on her knees toward the light, holding her hand in front of her.

Before she could even confirm her suspicions about the substance, her knee bumped a bare foot. Gasping for breath, her heart slamming against her chest, she leaned to the side to see around the corner of the couch.

Chuck Rawlings stared back at her with empty, mannequin eyes.

Chapter Ten

Coop stared out at the sea of pale, worried faces, wishing he could offer more assurances. "Are there any other questions?"

A redhead in the front row raised her hand and started speaking before he could call on her. "What about that pervert, Chuck Rawlings?"

"What about him, ma'am?"

"Have you checked him out? When my husband and I moved here four years ago, we looked at that sex offender database for Washington and he's on it." She folded her arms and fixed Coop with a steely stare.

"We've investigated him thoroughly, ma'am. He's clear."

"And the others in that database? Because we have more than Rawlings in the area now." A big man standing in the back shoved off the wall he'd been leaning against. "When Evergreen moved in here, they brought all their problems with 'em. I have to wait at that damned signal now on the main drag for close to a minute and the mayor won't respond to my emails."

A man in the front wearing a suit cranked his head around. "Yeah, among the problems Evergreen brought were more money for the schools and an increase in your property values. Even those ramshackle cabins near the woods are going for close to a quarter mil."

"Whose place are you calling ramshackle." The man in the back puffed out his chest.

"Stop." Coop held up his hands. "We're not here to discuss those issues. Follow the precautions on the flyer you picked up at the door. Most of the suggestions are common sense. I just wanted to assure you tonight that my department and the FBI are doing all we can right now to find out what happened to those children."

Someone in the crowd snorted and a few others coughed. Coop gritted his teeth.

"If there's nothing else, I'm sure we'd all like to collect our children, hug them tightly and head home."

Before anyone could start the Evergreen argument again, Mrs. Stoker, the principal, started clapping. "Thank you, Sheriff Sloane. We appreciate your presentation tonight. Let's start putting our newfound vigilance to practice. When you pick up your child from his or her classroom, please show the teacher your driver's license or other photo ID. I do realize most of the teachers know you, but let's turn these safety procedures into habits."

As the parents started shuffling out of the room and Coop was thanking Mrs. Stoker, his phone started going off in his pocket.

He held up his finger. "Hold that thought, Meg."

He plunged his hand into his pocket and withdrew his buzzing phone. The display indicated the call was coming from the station and it was the third call within the last minute.

Maybe someone had good news about those kids. "Coop here. What's up?"

"Coop, it's Payton. We have a dead body."

Coop's heart skipped a beat. "Not…"

"Not the kids, no." Payton sucked in a breath. "It's Chuck Rawlings."

"Rawlings? What happened?" Coop turned away from Mrs. Stoker, cupping his hand around his mouth.

"The officers on the scene aren't sure yet. He died from blunt force trauma. Could've been an accident."

"Are you telling me it could be murder?"

"'Fraid so, and that Timberline Trio lady found his body."

This time it felt like his heart had done a full somersault. "Kendall Rush? Kendall found him? Where, for God's sake?"

"In his house."

"Why the hell was Kendall in Rawlings's house?"

Payton paused a couple of beats. "Don't know. Don't know what to tell you, Coop."

Coop ended the call and made a beeline to the classroom where Steffi's age group had gathered during his talk to the parents. Luckily Britt and Rob were still there collecting Genevieve.

Coop tousled Steffi's curls and kissed the top of her head. "I just got an emergency call from the station. Can you take Steffi home with you tonight?"

Genevieve clapped her hands. "Please, Mom."

"Of course, Coop." Rob's gaze shifted to the two girls hugging. "Is it…"

"Something else. I really appreciate it. I'll pick her up when I'm done."

He had his police SUV at the school and drove out to Rawlings's place as if the man could still be saved, but he could spare very few thoughts about Rawlings. What had Kendall been doing in Rawlings's cabin?

He pulled up behind the police cruiser in the driveway. The rotating lights bathing the figures on the porch in red and blue. He squinted at Kendall on the bottom step, clutching something to her chest.

As he drew closer, his boots crunching the gravel on the driveway, the bundle in Kendall's arms squirmed and yapped. She had Rawlings's mutt in a firm grip as she talked to Officer Stevens.

She lifted her head to watch his approach, and then buried her face in the dog's fur.

Coop reached her in two long strides. "What happened? What were you doing here, Kendall?"

"R-Rawlings wanted to meet me. He left me a note." She rested her chin on top of the dog's head.

"So, you just came out here on your own?"

Out of the corner of his eye, Coop noticed Stevens's round eyes and his mouth hanging slightly ajar.

Coop dragged a hand through his hair and started over. "Did you call the county coroner's office, Stevens?"

"Yes, sir. The van's on its way. Paulson and Unger are inside with the body, taking pictures and checking out the scene."

"What do you think from your initial assessment? Accident or…homicide?"

Kendall's breath hissed between her teeth. "Homicide? Murder? He fell. Didn't he just fall over and hit his head?"

Coop raised an eyebrow at Stevens.

"Sir, he could've fallen and hit his head on the corner of a table."

"You called county Homicide along with the coroner?"

"Yes, sir."

"Stay here. I'm going to go inside and have a look." Coop placed a hand on Kendall's back and the little dog growled at him. "Looks like you have a protector. Where'd you find him?"

"He greeted me at the front door, which was open a crack. H-he had blood on his paws." She scratched the pooch under the chin and the tag on his collar jingled. "His name is Buddy."

"Okay, stay here with Buddy and Officer Stevens. Stevens, you wait for the county boys to get here."

Although he wanted to stay and question Kendall himself, he edged into Rawlings's house and dropped his gaze to the scuffed wood floor. The officers had put tags next to the bloody paw prints and a pair of slippers that looked like they'd been yanked from the deceased's feet—most likely the work of Buddy.

Deputy Unger came from the back room. "Hey, Coop. I was checking out the back windows for any evidence of a break-in."

"Anything?"

"Locked up tight."

"Ms. Rush said the front door was ajar when she got here."

Unger chewed his lip. "He could've been letting in some air, or maybe he felt bad, went to the front door for help, staggered back to the couch and then fell over."

"That's quite a scenario."

"For all we know, the guy had a heart attack and died from that instead of the blow to the head." Unger shrugged.

Coop eyed the blood pooling on the floor beneath Rawlings's head. "Maybe, but that wound was probably enough to kill him."

"I guess we'll find out from the autopsy."

Coop reached across and flicked aside the curtain at the front window. "The county coroner and Homicide just pulled up."

Coop and his officers spent the next hour going over details with the homicide detectives while another detective questioned Kendall. He wanted to be with her during the questioning, but he couldn't swing it.

When the detective finished with Kendall, she poked her head into the cabin. "Is it okay if I leave now?"

The lead detective answered. "Of course, Ms. Rush. We may call with a few more questions in the next couple of days, and we do have your contact info in Phoenix, right?"

"Yes." Her gaze shifted to Coop, and her eyebrows lifted.

He excused himself from the huddle and drew up beside her, taking her arm. "Are you okay to drive home by yourself?"

"I'm fine. I'm taking Buddy with me. I already put him in the truck. Detective Ross said it was okay."

"Poor little guy doesn't have anywhere else to go

except the pound. I should be finished up here in the next ten minutes and then I'm going to drop by your place, okay?"

"I know." She cupped her hand around her mouth and whispered. "We haven't had one minute to talk privately."

His pulse ticked up a notch. Did that mean she had more to tell him? "I'll be at your house as soon as I can."

That happened to be fifteen minutes. The coroner loaded the body and the homicide detectives loaded their baggies of evidence. "We'll keep in touch, Sheriff Sloane." Detective Ross scratched his chin. "Timberline is sure seeing its share of trouble to close out the year."

"Yeah, and we still have three months to go."

He hightailed it to Kendall's place, blowing out a breath when he saw her truck parked in front. He hadn't wanted to let her out of his sight.

She met him at the door with Buddy wrapped in a towel and tucked beneath her arm.

He leveled a finger at the dog. "Did you give him a bath already?"

"He had Rawlings's blood on his paws."

"Did you get it off?"

"Most of it." She swung the door open for him and placed Buddy on the floor. "Coffee?"

"No. I want to know why Rawlings asked you to his place."

"He left a note on my windshield tonight." She spread her hands. "I turned it over to the detective who questioned me."

"Of course. They'll be handling the investigation. We don't have the resources or manpower for what could be a homicide. If it proves to be an accident, we'll close out the case. What did the note say?"

"Rawlings wrote that he knew something about the pink ribbon."

He rubbed his chin. "How easy was that to explain to the detective?"

"Let's just say his eyes started to glaze over after about five minutes into my explanation."

"You should've told me, Kendall. You should've waited for me."

She took his hand. "Let's sit down."

They settled next to each other on the worn-out sofa in front of the cold fireplace.

"I was anxious to find out what Rawlings knew, and I really didn't think he posed any danger to me. I mean, he had sex with two teenage girls thirty years ago."

"That's what we know about, anyway." He stretched his legs out in front of him, his knee brushing hers. "Do you believe him? Do you think he had information?"

"He'd been watching me the night before in town."

"What?" He jerked his head toward her. "You didn't tell me that."

"I forgot. It happened after you and Steffi left the restaurant. I was walking back to my car, and he was sort of tracking me from across the street and then nodded at me right before I got in the truck."

"If he had this information, why didn't he tell you then?"

"I have no idea. Maybe he didn't want other people

to see him talking to me. Maybe he thought I'd freak out if he approached me. I mean, he is the town pariah."

"Was. The town will have to find a new pariah."

She clasped her hands between her knees. "Do you think someone killed him to stop him from telling me about the ribbon?"

"It's a possibility, and if that's what happened it's the kidnapper who left you the ribbon and the kidnapper who killed Rawlings. If someone was playing a prank on you with the ribbon, that's not motive enough for murder."

She shivered beside him, and he pressed his shoulder against hers. "It's all speculation, Kendall. It could all be a coincidence that Rawlings died of a heart attack or a stroke or a fall on the very night he invited you over."

"Some coincidence. Looks like the good citizens of Timberline are right—I am some sort of unlucky talisman."

Buddy pawed at her ankles, and Coop patted his head. "Buddy doesn't think so...and neither do I."

Kendall scooped Buddy into her lap and dropped her head to Coop's shoulder. "I'm not sure what I'd do without you here, Coop."

He draped his arm across her shoulders, and Buddy nipped at his fingers dangling close to Kendall's breast.

He laughed. "I think Buddy wants to be your bodyguard and won't stand for any intruders."

She tugged on Buddy's ear. "He saved me as much as I saved him. Having him there gave me something to concentrate on other than Chuck Rawlings's dead body."

Coop twirled a lock of Kendall's dark hair around

his finger. "So, we have a kidnapper who snatched two children, taunted two family members from the previous kidnapping case and then murdered a local man who had some information about a pink ribbon."

"My question is why?" Kendall scratched beneath Buddy's chin. "Why not just abduct the children and move on. Why continue to leave possible evidence?"

Coop's phone buzzed and he checked a text message from Britt. "Murderers do taunt law enforcement and don't always act rationally. Sometimes they even want to be caught."

"I hope the FBI can oblige him. And I hope we're dealing with a kidnapper only and not a killer." She hugged the dog to her chest.

Lucky little bastard.

"Where's Steffi tonight?"

"With Britt and Rob. I just got a text. She's already fast asleep."

"How'd the talk go? Were you able to reassure the parents?"

"Not much. It would've been better if Agent Maxfield had given the talk. The FBI is keeping me out of the loop and I didn't have much info to give the parents about those pictures or the progress of the investigation."

"That must be tough. Are you sure you're cut out for small-town policing?"

"Good question. We moved here because we thought a small town would be better for Alana's anxiety and depression. That didn't work, and I told you Steffi isn't happy with all the rain."

Buddy sprang from her lap. Brushing her hands together, she turned to face Coop. "I know I haven't known you long, Coop, but it seems to me you're not happy playing second fiddle to the FBI on the kidnapping case and you're not happy playing second fiddle to the county detectives on a possible homicide."

His lips quirked into a smile. "You haven't known me long, but you know me well."

"I'd better let you go." She stretched her arms over her head. "I need to find a place for Buddy to sleep tonight, and I have someone coming by tomorrow morning to start the yard work."

"You found someone?"

"Annie Foster found someone for me—Gary Binder."

"The ex-con?" A muscle at the corner of his mouth jumped. "You're hiring Gary Binder to clear your weeds?"

"I-it's not like he murdered someone. He was a junkie, and he's off the stuff now."

"Because he told you he was?" He shook his head. "As a therapist, you should know better."

"I seriously doubt he's any kind of danger to me, and he'll be working outside so he's not going to be stealing anything. I already told him he could have Aunt Cass's tools in the shed."

"I'll be around for a while tomorrow finishing up your security system in case he gets any ideas." He pushed up from the sagging sofa and shuffled his feet so he wouldn't step on Buddy. "Was Gary Binder living in Timberline at the time of your sister's kidnapping?"

"He was here. He was in his early twenties, a high school dropout." Folding her arms, she hunched her shoulders. "Are you implying that he could've been involved?"

"Anything's a possibility. I'll check the old case files to see if the FBI ever questioned him."

"It's not like he was in prison for twenty-five years and just got out to do another round of kidnappings. From what I understand, he's been in and out of jail for years."

"If Binder's going to be working around here, it's safer to check him out."

When she got to the front door, she tilted her head to the side. "Security system, personnel background checks. Have you become my private security guard?"

He touched a finger to her bottom lip. "Are you complaining?"

Her lips parted on a sigh. "I can use all the help I can get—for as long as I'm in Timberline."

And just like that, she reminded him that whatever they had between them was fleeting and temporary. She seemed to accept that fact—why couldn't he?

Chapter Eleven

The following morning, Gary Binder showed up at ten o'clock on the dot. Would someone still using be so prompt?

He leaned his bike against a tree trunk and rubbed his hands against the legs of his worn jeans. "I'm ready to get started."

She discussed the scope of the job with him again and his salary. "Deal?"

"Deal." He shook her hand. "Did you hear about old Chuck Rawlings? He fell and cracked his head open—probably plastered."

So, the cops, or someone, was spreading the accident story. "Was he a drinker?"

"Oh, yeah."

Buddy launched himself against the screen door inside and started yapping.

"You have a dog?"

"Actually, he was Chuck's dog."

Gary's eyes bugged out of their sockets like a cartoon character. "How'd you wind up with Chuck's dog?"

"It's a long story." She waved one hand in the air. "I can let him out here so he'll stop barking."

"Don't...please." Two red spots formed on Gary's pale cheeks. "I don't much like dogs, ma'am."

"Oh, okay, as long as you don't mind the barking."

"I'd rather have the barking than the biting."

"I don't think Buddy bites, but I don't know him all that well, so I'll keep him away from you." She pointed toward the shed. "Let's have a look at the tools."

She plucked a key from the large, silver ring that sported many more. "I think this is it. It's the only one small enough for a padlock."

The key fit and she swung open the door of the shed as the rusty hinges squealed. "No lights. Let's get the other door."

Gary reached around inside and lifted the stake that held the second door in place.

With both doors open wide, the daylight streamed into the close quarters, both sides lined with shelves and tools hanging from the walls. A lawn mower and weed whacker took up one corner.

"Looks like enough to get started." Gary hooked his thumbs in his belt loops.

"Not sure there's any gasoline for that lawn mower."

"I can take care of that, ma'am."

"Then I'll leave it in your hands." She pulled some cash and the keys to the truck from her pocket. "Buy what you need and take the truck to get it."

He carefully counted the money before folding it up and putting it in the front pocket of his jeans. "There's eighty bucks there. I'll give you your change and receipts at the end of the day."

"That'll be fine." She almost said something about his need to show his trustworthiness, but it was just that—a need. He had to go through that for his own peace of mind and well-being—probably part of his road to recovery.

A black truck turned into the drive and her heart leaped for a brief minute and then landed with a thud when she saw the driver. Wyatt waved out his window instead of Coop.

He scrambled from the truck and strode toward her, a big smile splitting his baby face. "How's it going, Kendall?"

She raised her eyebrows. What a difference a couple of days made, or maybe he'd unburdened himself to his new therapist. "It's going. I'm getting ready for the estate sale this weekend and Rebecca already got a couple of bites on the house."

"Really?" Wyatt pushed his baseball cap farther back on his head. "For this old place? Makes me think I should list my folks' place."

"With Evergreen creating more and more jobs, the real estate prices will keep going up."

"I hope so. Did you hear about Rawlings?"

"I did. I'm the one who found him."

"What?"

Wyatt's surprise seemed forced. The word must already be out that she'd discovered Rawlings and Gary just missed the memo.

"I went over there to see him about something—his dog—and I found Chuck on the floor." If Dr. Shipman had Wyatt feeling better about life, she didn't want to bring him down with reminders about the kidnappings—past or present.

"That's not what you want to find when you go to

someone's house." Wyatt rubbed his chin. "I heard he was drunk and took a spill."

"That seems to be the general consensus. He was bleeding from the head, but of course he could've had a heart attack and hit his head on the way down."

"That's rough." He pointed to Buddy furiously pawing at the screen door. "I see you got the dog, though."

"Buddy. I'd let him out, but Gary doesn't like dogs."

"I don't like them, either. Gary?"

"Binder." She jerked her thumb over her shoulder. "He's going to be clearing out the weeds and shrubs."

Wyatt dropped his chin to his chest. "Do you think that's a good idea, Kendall? Don't you remember Binder when we were kids and he was the town punk and druggie?"

"Vaguely, but he's clean and sober now."

"That's what they all say. Look at Rawlings."

"I'm not sure Rawlings ever claimed to be clean and sober."

"He went back and forth, like they all do."

Wyatt should know since his father had descended into alcoholism when Stevie went missing, just as her own mother had descended into madness. The kidnappings had created ripples of misery that had gone on for years.

"Well, Annie Foster recommended him and I'm giving him a chance."

He shrugged. "Since she's a fortune-teller or something, I guess she'd know."

Hadn't Wyatt lived among the Quileute long enough to know the shamans didn't consider themselves fortune-tellers? "I think you mean her cousin Scarlett Easton, and she's a shaman, not a fortune-teller."

"Whatever. Too bad Scarlett's not here to find those kids."

"I don't think she does that sort of thing."

Gary dragged a wheelbarrow from the back and she and Wyatt jumped.

Crossing his arms, Wyatt called out, "You know what you're doing here, Binder?"

A twist of anger claimed Gary's face for a second before he retreated back into his obsequious persona. "Yes, sir. It don't take an expert landscaper or an expert *plumber* to clear out some brush."

Wyatt's hands balled into fists against his biceps, and Kendall stepped into the space between the two men as Gary started whistling an off-key tune. "Can I do something for you, Wyatt?"

"I just wanted to thank you for being a friend, Kendall." He rolled his shoulders and tilted his head from side to side, cracking his neck.

He must've seen Dr. Shipman, who must've told him not to blab about his sessions all over town.

"Anytime, Wyatt. We do have a bond, even though it's one we'd both rather forget."

Another black truck pulled up, and Coop honked his horn twice.

Wyatt squinted at Coop's truck even though not one ray of sunshine had broken through the cloud cover yet. "What's Coop doing here? Is he gonna talk to you about Rawlings?"

"I doubt it, since he called out the homicide detectives from county."

Wyatt's gaze tracked between her and Coop, now getting out of his truck, trying to put two and two together.

She *wished* there was more going on between her and her hunky bodyguard, but she'd have to be satisfied with meaningful looks and accidental skin-on-skin contact. As a single dad, Coop probably didn't go for one-night stands and love 'em and leave 'em hot nights. And she'd be the one doing the loving and leaving, since she had no intention of staying in Timberline for Coop or anyone else.

Coop's boots crunched the gravel as he approached them. "Looks like a regular convention here." He nodded at Gary.

Wyatt gripped the bill of his baseball cap, tugging it down over his forehead. "I just dropped by to see if Kendall was all right after finding Rawlings last night."

"I'm wondering the same thing." Coop quirked an eyebrow at her.

"I'm fine." She shifted her gaze away from Wyatt. So, he *had* known she was the one who found Rawlings, or he was just covering in front of Coop.

"Good to hear. I gotta go now." Wyatt shook Coop's hand and headed for his truck.

"I have about an hour free." He spread his arms, opening his jacket and indicating his khaki uniform. "I think I can finish installing the security system in that time."

"You're not doing this on your lunch break, are you? And when do those days off start?"

"It's a break. We don't have to call it lunch, and I'll take the time off when I need it."

"The least I can do is get you some lunch. I'll pick up some sandwiches at Dina's Deli." She jerked her chin toward Gary. "Between you and me, he could use some meat on his bones."

Coop tipped his head back and laughed as he marched toward the house. "Beware of stray dogs."

He swung open the screen door before she could warn him about Buddy, and the little dog didn't waste any time escaping. He bounded from the porch and made a beeline toward Gary.

As Gary backed up into a bush, Buddy scampered back and forth in front of him, stopping every few seconds to bark up at him.

"Buddy!" She jogged over and picked up the squirming animal with both hands. "You need some obedience training. Sorry, Gary."

"That's okay." He edged away from her and Buddy. "I got bit by a dog once and never liked 'em since."

"That's understandable." She tucked Buddy under one arm and scolded him all the way to the front door.

Coop looked up from the boxes and wires spread in front of him on the table. "What was all that about?"

"Buddy went nuts on Gary, and Gary doesn't like dogs."

Coop snorted. "Probably had a few run-ins with some nasty mutts when he was busy breaking into people's homes."

"You and Wyatt just can't cut the guy a break." She picked up a wire and twirled it around. "You don't still suspect he had something to do with the Timberline Trio case, do you?"

"Haven't dismissed the idea yet, but I haven't had time to check him out in the old files, either."

Buddy put two paws on the coffee table where Coop had the parts to the security system laid out and grabbed a piece in his mouth and took off.

"Buddy!"

"You'd better get that piece outta that mutt's mouth." Coop lunged toward the spinning, yapping dog, but Buddy weaved between his legs and scampered toward the hallway.

Kendall followed him into the bedroom where he'd jumped onto the bed, a white piece of plastic between his paws and clamped in his jaws.

"You naughty boy." She slipped her fingers into his mouth and pried the piece from his teeth.

"You got it?" Coop filled the doorway, his hands braced against the doorjamb as if he could block Buddy's exit.

She held up the mangled piece, wet with Buddy's slobber. "Was it important?"

"Just the motion sensor." He ran a hand over his mouth. "I can put everything else in, but I'm going to have to go back to Port Angeles tomorrow to replace this part."

"Perfect." She dropped the piece on her nightstand and wiped her fingers on her jeans. "I have to pay a visit to my online auctioneer. We can go together."

"Do you trust me?" He walked to the bed and swept the sensor from the nightstand and growled at Buddy. "I kinda made a mess of our trip last time."

"I trust you. We'll do it right this time, but I'm just warning you." She crossed her two index fingers in front of her face. "I'm going to drop in on Dr. Shipman, and it has nothing to do with you. She actually has a referral for me in Phoenix."

He ducked his head. "Don't rub it in. I made a total ass of myself."

"You'll get no argument from me."

"I didn't think I would." He picked up Buddy with one hand and deposited him in her arms. "Now, keep an eye on this nuisance while I wire up your security system."

Holding Buddy, Kendall followed Coop to the front door and watched him lean the ladder against the house.

She put her lips close to Buddy's furry ear and whispered, "You're a good bodyguard, but Coop's even better."

THE FOLLOWING MORNING, Kendall stood on the porch and surveyed Gary's progress.

Sensing her scrutiny, Gary looked up from hoeing a patch of dirt. "Everything okay, ma'am? I thought I'd turn up this area here and then start on the bushes lining the driveway."

"Looks fine. You're doing a good job, Gary. Do you want me to leave you some leftovers for lunch?"

"No, thank you." He indicated a small, soft-sided cooler and a container of water next to his bike. "I brought my own lunch today."

"All right." She waved at Coop pulling up in his truck. "I'm heading to Port Angeles today, but don't worry about Buddy. I penned him up on the patio in the back."

"I'll just take care of business out front."

She nodded and practically skipped to Coop's truck. She and Coop planned to take care of their own business this morning in Port Angeles and try lunch again.

When she hopped in the truck, Coop narrowed his eyes and stared at Gary. "You sure it's okay to leave Binder here alone?"

"I locked up the house." She snapped her seat belt in place. "He's actually doing a pretty good job. Don't you think so?"

"Looks okay."

"Has he been causing any trouble around here since his last stint in jail?"

"He hasn't been around much since I moved here. The guys in the department told me about him, said his mother still lives in the area and that he comes and goes when he visits her. As far as I can remember, he hasn't had any arrests."

"He'll be fine. Besides, I have Buddy to stand guard, and he's terrified of the dog."

"That mutt is not terrifying, but he is a menace." Coop tapped a box on the console.

"Is the sensor in there?"

"Yeah, and I'm hoping they'll replace it for me at no charge."

"If there is one, I'll cover it." She turned down the radio. "Any news on Rawlings?"

"Not yet. Homicide is running a toxicology report, and the medical examiner is going to do an autopsy. If they can rule out accidental or natural causes, Homicide will step up its investigation."

She shivered and cranked on the heater. "Are they looking into my story about the pink ribbon?"

"They're taking it into consideration, but they're not all that excited about it being a motive for murder."

"Okay, that's it." She pretended to zip her lips. "I'd like to enjoy at least one day when I'm not talking about pranks, kidnappings and murder."

"And since this is officially a day off for me, I'm with you on that."

They kept to their word for the rest of the drive, at least in spirit. Kendall never could quite banish the gloomy thoughts that had dogged her since returning to Timberline. But then, Timberline and gloomy thoughts went hand in hand for her, and that's why she couldn't wait to return to Arizona—except for the thought of leaving this man behind.

As they pulled into town, Coop turned to her. "I'll come with you to the online auction store, and then I think it would be better if we parted ways. I'll drop you off at Dr. Shipman's, and then I'll head to the security shop."

"I think you just want to check out the Elvis boots." She punched him in the arm.

The Elvis boots were gone when they got to the shop, so Coop wandered around looking at the other odds and ends while Kendall went over final pricing with Jessa.

"I guess that's it, Jessa. Thanks for everything."

"No problem. I think this stuff will sell."

Brushing her hands together, she stepped onto the sidewalk with Coop. "Glad that's over with."

When they got back in the truck, Coop gripped the

steering wheel with both hands. "You know, when my wife died, I couldn't get rid of her stuff fast enough—clothes, toiletry items, even the foods she liked—I didn't feel guilty until some people started giving me strange looks. But I guess you and I are alike…lose the stuff that causes you pain and move on. Isn't that how you feel about your aunt's things? The collections? The house itself?"

"I do, and it's not like I'm ever going to forget my twin. I will never forget Kayla, but I have my own memories of her in here." She thumped a fist against her chest. "I don't need the stuff that reminds me of the day I lost her forever."

He cranked on the engine. "Exactly."

Coop drove the short distance to Dr. Shipman's office and pulled up to the curb.

Kendall slid from the truck and went around to the driver's side as Coop powered down the window. "Do you want to try the same place for lunch, or would that be bringing back bad memories?"

He chuckled. "I think we can make some new memories there. Give me a call when you're done. I'll head back over here once I get this piece replaced, and I'll wait here if you're not ready."

"Got it." She stepped away from the truck and waved.

She walked toward the office while Coop's truck idled at the curb. She reached for the door, turning the handle, and a crack resounded in the distance. The stucco on the wall next to her shattered. A piece struck her cheek.

Her hand jerked to the sting on her face, and her

fingers met moisture. As if in a dream, she stared at the blood on her fingertips.

Coop shouted behind her. "Get down! Get down! Someone's shooting."

She turned her head just in time to see Coop launching his body at her. Another crack split the air and she lost all the breath in her lungs.

Chapter Twelve

Coop landed on top of Kendall, and she grunted with the force of the pressure.

A door opened and a woman screamed. More shouts and screams from outside the office.

"What happened? What are you doing?"

Coop glanced into the face of the woman he blamed for Alana's suicide.

She recoiled and clapped both hands over her mouth, her eyes wide and glassy. "Mr. Sloane!"

Kendall's body jerked beneath his and he rolled off her. His heart slammed against his chest when he saw the blood staining her cheek. Had he reacted too slowly?

"Kendall? Are you all right?" He rose to his knees and shouted at Dr. Shipman. "Call 9-1-1."

"Wh-what happened?"

"Someone was shooting outside."

"Oh, my God."

"Kendall?"

Her eyelids flew open and she panted out jerky words. "What. Happened out. There?"

"Did you get hit?" He ran his hands down her arms. "Your face is bleeding."

"The stucco. The stucco hit me."

A man poked his head in the office door. "Is everyone okay in here?"

"We're fine. Out there?"

"Everyone hit the ground or took cover. Someone saw him on top of the building across the street."

Adrenaline blasted through Coop's system, and he jumped to his feet. "Dr. Shipman, can you help Kendall?"

"Of course, and the police are on the way."

He couldn't wait for the Port Angeles police, not if a killer was on the loose.

He helped Kendall to the love seat in the waiting room and tucked her hair behind her ear. "Stay here with Dr. Shipman."

Gripping his arm, she said, "Be careful, Coop."

With his weapon in his hand, he hit the sidewalk. "Which building?"

His gaze glued to the gun, a man pointed to a white, three-story building across the street.

"I'm a cop. When the Port Angeles police get here, tell them I went after the shooter."

Coop sprinted across the street in case the guy started shooting again. He hugged the side of the building, and then slipped in the front door.

A few people cowered near a potted plant in the corner, and Coop flashed his badge. "I'm a cop. Stay inside. The shooter was spotted on the roof of this building. Did you see anyone coming down and leaving the building?"

They all shook their heads, and one woman pointed to the ceiling. "You can get to the roof from the stairwell around the corner, past the elevators."

He headed for the stairwell and jogged upward, bursting through the door to the rooftop. Crouching, he made his way to the edge of the building that faced the street and Dr. Shipman's office. Sirens wailed, closer and closer.

He studied the gravel on the surface of the roof and noted several disturbances, although they could've been recent or from days or weeks before. He crouched, the gravel shifting beneath his feet, and ran his hand along the edge of the roof—plenty of room to hide and aim a rifle.

His gaze swept the surface, but the shooter must've collected his shell casings before he left. Coop sniffed the air and detected a faint scent of gunpowder. Or was that his imagination?

The door behind him crashed and a female voice shouted. "Place your weapon on the ground and put your hands up."

Coop complied with the officer's orders.

"Turn around, slowly."

He turned with his hands raised in the air. "I'm Sheriff Cooper Sloane from Timberline, ma'am."

"Badge?"

"In my pocket." He dipped his chin toward his chest, indicating the front pocket of his flannel shirt.

Another officer burst onto the roof behind the female cop.

Without shifting her aim, she said, "Says he's Sheriff Sloane from Timberline. Badge is in his front pocket."

The male officer had his weapon trained on Coop, as well. "Take it out of your pocket nice and easy and toss it toward us."

Coop followed his instructions and once they got a look at his badge, they lowered their guns.

"I was across the street when the shooting started and someone said the shots came from up here."

The first cop on the scene answered. "Did you find anything?"

"No, and nobody in the building saw him leave."

"There's a back exit from the stairwell. He may have gone that way." The male officer holstered his weapon. "We have officers combing the area."

"I'll leave you two to canvas the roof. I left my friend down there. One of the shots came close to her head."

They asked him a few more questions and let him leave. By the time he got back to Dr. Shipman's office, the EMTs had Kendall bandaged up and sitting on the back of the ambulance.

"Are you okay? How's the face?" He leaned against the ambulance door.

She touched a fingertip to the edge of the white square on her cheek. "It's okay. I'm fine. You didn't find anything on the roof?"

"I didn't. The Port Angeles police are up there now." He circled his finger in the air. "Did anyone else see anything?"

"Just the few people who'd claimed to see someone on that roof at about the same time the shots were fired. The police already questioned me, but I was useless. I didn't even know what was going on."

"Then I tackled you." He brushed a hand over the smooth hair on the top of her head. "I think I knocked the wind out of you."

She caught his hand. "I think you saved my life."

Giving her fingers a squeeze, he asked, "Were any more shots besides those two fired?"

"The two that were fired at me, you mean?" She shook her head. "I don't think so. All anyone reported hearing were the two shots."

An EMT returned to the back of the ambulance, peeling off a pair of plastic gloves. "All your vitals check out, miss. You're free to leave, but remember to remove your bandage in a few hours to clean your wound."

Coop took Kendall's arm as she hopped off the back of the van. "Do the officers need to question you anymore?"

"They told me I could leave after I gave them my contact info. Like I said, I was no use whatsoever."

"I'm just glad you're okay." He cupped her face in his palms, and her soft hair brushing the backs of his hands made him ache somewhere deep inside. "When I heard that first shot and saw the wall next to you explode, my heart stopped."

"Kendall, how are you feeling?"

Coop raised his eyes above Kendall's head and met the gaze of Dr. Shipman. His gut knotted as he remembered their last encounter, the one before he crashed on her office doorstep on top of Kendall.

Kendall disengaged herself from him and turned to face Dr. Shipman. "I feel okay, Jules, still a little weak in the knees."

"I can't believe that happened here. Must be some very disturbed individual, and I hope the police find him before he has a chance to do it again."

"Do you think he will?" Kendall crossed her arms, hugging her purse to her chest. "He sure gave up quickly. Two shots and done. Isn't that unusual, Coop?"

A sharp pinprick of fear jabbed the base of his skull, and he rubbed the back of his neck. "I don't know what's usual or unusual in these circumstances. He could've gotten spooked when those people turned and pointed at the roof."

"I hope it spooked him enough to scare him out of these parts." Dr. Shipman hunched her shoulders. "Kendall, you're probably too shaken up to discuss that other matter. I can give you a call or we can interface over the computer."

"Of course. Thanks for your help, Jules."

"I'm just glad my office provided you some shelter." She gave Kendall a quick hug. "Have a nice trip back to Phoenix, and I'll be in touch."

"Thanks, Jules."

Dr. Shipman nodded toward Coop. "Sheriff Sloane."

Coop unclenched his jaw. "Thank you, Dr. Shipman."

Kendall blew out a long breath. "Lunch?"

"Are you kidding?"

"Not at all. Remember those two glasses of wine I had the last time we lunched at the Pelican's Nest? Well, I could use a couple more."

"Aren't pelicans supposed to bring bad luck to sailors? Maybe we should change it up."

She pinched his arm. "That's an albatross, as in you don't want one around your neck."

"I don't think I want a pelican around my neck, either."

Kendall started laughing, doubled over and then started snorting.

"Are you getting hysterical?" He rubbed a circle on her back just as a news van pulled up and discharged a reporter and a cameraman.

Coop grabbed Kendall's arm. "Unless you want to be on the six o'clock news, I suggest we head for the Pelican's Nest or even the Albatross's Nest if that keeps you laughing."

She wiped a few tears from the corners of her eyes and matched him step for step back to his truck, which it seems they'd left a lifetime ago.

He started the engine, did a U-turn and drove toward the water.

When they were seated with a couple of drinks in front of them, Coop took Kendall's hand and started toying with her fingers. "Out with it, Kendall. What were you thinking back there at Dr. Shipman's office? What were you thinking about this sniper?"

"I think you know." She took a gulp of wine as if to fortify her courage. "Why shoot at someone about to go into a building? Why two shots only? Why did the shots stop when the first and only victim—" she raised her hand "—was pushed out of range?"

"You think the shots were meant for you." He pinged his fingernail against his beer bottle and watched a rivulet of moisture run down the glass.

"Are you telling me that thought never crossed your mind?"

"I was too busy going after the shooter to consider it."

"But now that you've had a chance to consider it?" She took another swig of wine from her glass, leaving a pink lipstick print on the rim.

He wanted to ignore the feeling of dread sketching a cold trail in his veins but if Kendall had the guts to face the truth head-on, he owed it to her to come along for the ride. "I know strange things have been happening to you, but I still can't put my finger on a motive. I've turned it over a few times, and haven't come up with a good reason why the kidnapper would want to kill you—unless he's the same man who took your sister and he's afraid you'll remember."

"What would be his motive for any of it? The ribbon? The mannequin? Burying those photos on my property?"

"Maybe he wants you to find the missing children, but it doesn't explain the shots fired"

She buried her chin in her palm. "I don't know, but I'm getting out of here."

His heart dropped with a thud and he made a big deal out of studying the menu. "Are you going to eat lunch first?"

"I'm not leaving right this minute." She flicked a finger at his menu. "But I'm going to get through the yard sale this weekend and then I'm leaving."

"Probably a good idea. Whatever's happening to you is tied to Timberline and those kidnappings. The sooner you get back to Phoenix, the better…for you."

She raised the menu to cover her face and responded in a muffled voice. "I think so, too. Have you heard anything from the FBI about the pictures or any evidence left at the burial sites?"

He held up his hand as the waiter approached, and they ordered their food.

Coop took a sip of his beer, and started picking at the foil label. "The FBI guys are tight-lipped when it comes to local law enforcement."

"It's been almost a month since those kids were taken, hasn't it?"

"Yeah, earlier in September."

"Maybe those pictures mean the kids are still alive. They looked kind of grungy, didn't they?" Kendall's eyebrows rose in a hopeful expression.

"They did, so maybe that's their condition after being held for three weeks." He entwined his fingers with her fidgeting ones. "The FBI is looking at other clues from the pictures, like the lighting, which is harsh and unnatural. They're also investigating where someone would get that newspaper with the Timberline Trio headline."

"That is odd. How would someone get ahold of that? I don't think even Aunt Cass had saved those papers, even though it seems like she saved everything else." She wrinkled her nose. "And actually I thought she had saved a pile of those."

"The FBI hasn't even determined yet if those are original newspapers or printouts or reprints. They could've come from anywhere."

"I guess." She tapped the window. "Have you even noticed the view today?"

He looked into the depths of her dark eyes. "I noticed the view."

A pink tinge touched her cheeks. "I meant the one out the window."

"That, too." His gaze shifted to the grayish-blue water lapping at the boats in the harbor. "We were going to have a stress-free day."

"Yeah, that lasted until the shooting started."

"The shooting's over and you're safe, so let's try to salvage the afternoon."

The waiter delivered their food as if on cue, and Coop flicked his napkin into his lap. "I'm rebooting the afternoon, starting now."

"I'll drink to that." She touched her wineglass to his bottle. "We'd better pick up the pace here if you're going to pick up Steffi from the Fletchers'."

"I'm only going to see her for a short time tonight. There's a birthday party sleepover, so I'm just there to be her chauffeur and personal assistant to make sure she packs everything."

"It seems like she spends a lot of time with Genevieve's family. Do you think you're using Britt as a substitute maternal figure for Steffi?" She swirled the wine in her glass, holding her breath.

Coop pinched the bridge of his nose. "It's not easy being a single dad to a little girl. Once Steffi started school and saw all the other moms, she seemed to want to spend more time at her friends' homes, homes with moms who had high heels and make-up and clothes for dress-up—and I let her. Does that make me a bad father?"

Kendall swallowed the lump in her throat. "Of course not."

"It wasn't always like that." A small smile played over his lips. "When she was a toddler, it was just the two of us—the zoo, the park, swimming lessons. The shift happened when she started school. Instead of spending time with me, she wanted to be with her friends. I suppose I screwed it all up."

She traced the knuckles of his clenched hand with her fingertip. "You didn't screw up anything. She'll gravitate back toward you."

"Thanks, Kendall."

"Besides, she seems well-adjusted." She slid her hand from his and then cupped it around a slice of lemon and squeezed it on her fish.

He lifted one shoulder. "Yeah, except for that irrational hatred for the rain—and she's in a bad place for that."

"I wouldn't necessarily call it an irrational hatred." Kendall wiped her hands on a napkin, and then traced a drop of moisture rolling down the window outside with her fingertip.

He stabbed a tomato with his fork. "Most kids don't pay attention to the weather one way or the other. Steffi was born here. You'd think she'd be used to it like all the other kids in Timberline. Did you even notice the weather here until you grew up and moved somewhere else?"

"I used to like the rain—the smell of it, the feel of it on my face, the taste of it on my tongue. I liked it until the cool temperatures and gray skies started getting depressing, and yes, that happened as I hit adolescence and started brooding on my lost twin."

"That had to be painful. I have a sister and as annoying as she is sometimes, I can't imagine losing her even though I don't see her often."

Kendall blinked back her emotions and sawed off a corner of her fish. "Why is that?"

"Her husband works for the State Department, and they live in Spain right now."

"Must be nice." She tilted her head to one side. "Did you have one of those idyllic childhoods with the family of four behind a white picket fence?"

"Guilty." He raised his hand. "That's why I was unprepared for my wife's...darkness."

She snapped her fingers in the air. "No more darkness today."

They finished their lunch, recovering from their rocky beginning just like they had the other day. Kendall was the type of woman he should've been with from the beginning—pragmatic, resilient, strong. The guilt leaped in his chest like a flame. Kendall would probably be the first one to tell him that Alana's depression didn't make her weak, just ill.

Before they left Port Angeles, Coop stopped by the security store and exchanged the damaged sensor for a new one.

On the way home, the sprinkles turned into rain.

Kendall sighed. "I hope it's not raining like this in Timberline. I was hoping Gary could finish the front today so I'd have a cleared-out space for the estate sale."

"We were supposed to have a respite from the rain

this weekend, so maybe this will clear up by the time we get back."

He was right. By the time they had pulled into Timberline, the dark clouds had thinned out, but Binder still hadn't finished the work.

"What the heck happened?" Kendall sat forward in her seat. "It doesn't look like he got much further than when I left."

"I'm not going to say I told you so." He parked his truck behind Kendall's. "His bike is gone."

"Damn. I thought the guy was sincere about wanting to get the job done." She jumped from the truck before he turned off the engine.

He joined her as she stood in the middle of the front yard, hands on her hips.

"I can finish it up for you—at least enough so you can put some tables out here for the estate sale."

"You need to finish the security system and, besides, you've already done enough." She kicked a rock with the toe of her boot. "I'm going to check on Buddy and release him from his prison."

Coop returned to his truck to get the new security sensor.

Then a high-pitched scream pierced the air and he dropped the bag and ran to Kendall.

He rounded the corner to the backyard and tripped to a stop as Kendall, her face ashen and her eyes like two black coals, held out Buddy in front of her.

"He's dead."

Chapter Thirteen

Kendall pressed the limp dog to her chest as a sob broke from her lips. This place. This house. Took everything from her.

Coop crouched beside her and wrapped his arms around her and Buddy. "I'm sorry. What happened to the little guy?"

She lifted her eyes, brimming with tears, to his face. "He was lying on his side in the pen. He had foam bubbling from his mouth."

"Still bubbling?" He took Buddy into his own arms and pressed his ear against the dog's body.

"Yeah." Her gaze scanned the patio within the pen and stumbled across a piece of lunch meat and a dried leaf.

"He's still alive, Kendall. He has a faint heartbeat." Coop sprang to his feet, Buddy in his arms. "If we can get him to Doc Washburn as soon as possible, he might have a chance."

Kendall dashed the tears from her face and staggered to her feet. "What are we waiting for?"

She followed Coop to his truck and slid into the passenger seat, where he transferred his bundle to her.

She cradled Buddy in her arms, whispering, "Hang on. Keep fighting, Buddy."

Coop's truck flew across the wet asphalt of the road and screeched to a stop in front of the local vet's office.

Kendall jumped from the truck and ran into the waiting room with Buddy against her shoulder. "We have an emergency. I came home and my dog was unresponsive and foaming at the mouth, but he's still breathing."

The receptionist pressed a button on an intercom attached to the wall. "Emergency in the front."

Within seconds, a tech burst through the swinging doors that led to the examination rooms. As he took Buddy from her arms, Kendall explained the dog's condition.

"Do you know if he ate something? Chewed on something?"

"There was a piece of meat and a leaf in the pen he was in."

Nodding, the tech backed into an examination room and said, "Wait out front. We'll do what we can."

Kendall stumbled back to the waiting room where Coop was on the phone, pacing across the floor.

"Do you need to go to Steffi?"

"It's not time yet. I was just checking up on her. She's at Genevieve's and they're helping Britt frost the birthday cake." He took her hands. "Did Doc Washburn say anything?"

"I didn't see him. A tech took Buddy into an exam room and asked me some questions." She grabbed his wrist. "Coop, there was a piece of bologna or something in the pen. I didn't give Buddy anything like that."

"Did you pick it up? Do you have it with you?"

"No. Should I go get it?" Her gaze darted to the swinging doors. "I don't want to leave him."

"Are you okay here alone? I can drive back and pick it up."

"Would you?" She pressed her lips against his knuckles. What would she do without this man by her side?

"Hang in there. I'll be back as soon as I can."

When Coop left, Kendall wandered around the waiting room picking up and discarding magazines.

After the receptionist assisted a customer with a cat carrier in hand, she turned to Kendall. "Was that your dog you brought in?"

"Yes. Buddy."

The receptionist cocked her head. "Wasn't that Chuck Rawlings's dog?"

"I...uh...adopted him."

"Okay. I thought so. We've seen Buddy before."

"For anything like this?"

"Not that I remember—just routine stuff. Do you know what happened to Chuck?"

"No idea. Heart attack?" Kendall shrugged. She wasn't about to reveal her suspicions to this curious receptionist. It would seem that she brought bad luck everywhere she went, not only to humans but animals.

Another forty minutes ticked by before Coop returned, a small plastic bag in hand. He dangled it from his fingers in the light. "A piece of bologna."

"Where did it come from?"

"It didn't fall from the sky. I wish I'd had the security system hooked up." He pressed the bag into her hand. "Do you want to give this to Washburn?"

She waved the plastic bag at the receptionist. "Buddy was eating this. Do you think Dr. Washburn wants to see it?"

"Absolutely. I'll call Blake up to get it."

She pressed the intercom again and the tech materialized in the waiting room. "Buddy, the dog that just came in? He may have been eating this."

"Okay, great."

"How's he doing? Do you have any news?"

"I'll let Dr. Washburn tell you. He's almost done and it looks like Buddy's going to pull through."

Kendall closed her eyes and covered her face. "Thank you."

Coop pressed a hand against the small of her back. "Sit down. You've been on the edge ever since we found Buddy, and your afternoon wasn't exactly a walk in the park, either."

She allowed him to propel her to a vinyl chair that squeaked when she dropped to the seat. "Someone poisoned him. Someone fed him tainted meat. And what happened to Gary?"

"Do you have his phone number?"

"The guy doesn't have a cell phone."

"He lives with his mother, Raylene Binder. We can call Raylene at home or drop by." Coop ran his knuckles along his stubble.

A pulse throbbed in her throat. "What are you thinking?"

"I'm wondering if Gary dislikes all dogs or just Buddy."

"And why would he just dislike Buddy?" She

flicked her tongue across her dry lips, suddenly unable to swallow.

"Because Buddy was there when Binder killed Rawlings."

Kendall sucked in a breath. "I had the same thought."

"And if Binder had a reason to kill Rawlings, it might just have to do with Rawlings's meeting with you." He drummed his fingers on the arm of the chair. "Did you ever check with Annie about whether or not she even talked to Binder? Maybe Annie came up with Binder's name because he approached her to put in a good word for him."

Kendall pressed her fingers to her temples. "This is too much. Do you think Binder took off after poisoning Buddy?"

"Look, this is all supposition at this point, Kendall. I'll need to find Binder first and talk to him."

"Ms. Rush?" Dr. Washburn stepped through the swinging doors, a clipboard tucked under his arm.

She popped up. "Yes?"

"Buddy's going to be fine. He's a little weak from getting his stomach pumped, so he just needs some rest and soft food for a day or two."

"Thank you. Was it poison?"

"Probably rat poison. I recommend using traps instead of poison if you have rats."

Coop placed a hand on her shoulder. "Did you test the piece of lunch meat that we brought in?"

"A preliminary test showed nothing on the meat, but that doesn't mean someone didn't wrap a cold cut around some poison." Dr. Washburn shoved his glasses up the bridge of his nose. "Is that what you think happened?"

"Possibly. Have you had any other cases of pet poisoning?"

"We have not, Sheriff, but as you might remember we had a rash of pet murders a few years back. Someone was shooting dogs and cats with a pellet gun."

Coop nodded. "I remember that. It stopped after about eight months."

"There was a string of those before you came here as sheriff. Those stopped as suddenly as they started, too." Dr. Washburn spread his hands. "Other than that, we haven't had any issues. I hope what happened to Buddy is not the start of another pet killing spree."

"I hope you're right." Kendall pressed a hand against her heart. "Can I take Buddy home now?"

"I think he'd like that."

As she settled the bill at the counter, the tech brought Buddy out, wrapped in a fuzzy blue blanket. His tail hanging out of the end, wagged weakly.

"Buddy!" She took the little dog in her arms and pressed her cheek against his head.

Coop led the way back to the truck. "I'm going to drop off you and Buddy, and then I'm going to pay a visit to Raylene Binder."

"I'm coming with you."

"And Buddy?"

Scratching the dog's ear, she said, "I could tuck him at home."

"I've got an idea. The Fletchers are dog people and I want to see Steffi before she goes to the sleepover, so let's leave Buddy there where he can get lots of attention."

"Great idea."

As Coop drove to the Fletchers' house, Buddy seemed to perk up. Kendall stroked the pup's soft fur and rubbed his belly. "Who could harm a pet?"

"You heard Dr. Washburn. There are a lot of sick people out there."

"As evidenced by the kidnappings."

"Sometimes the same urge that drives someone to harm an animal compels them to harm a human. A lot of serial killers started out practicing their art on pets."

She swallowed. "And they walk among us like normal people."

By the time they reached the Fletchers', Buddy was licking her fingers and thumping his tail. "You're in for a treat. You get to recuperate with kids."

Britt answered the door and squealed when she saw Buddy poke his head from the blanket. "He's adorable."

Steffi and Genevieve were soon crowding in, tugging at the blanket to get a peek at Buddy.

"Sit down, Steffi. I'll put him in your lap."

Coop's daughter plopped down on the sofa, and Kendall placed the dog in her arms.

Steffi touched her nose to his. "He's cute. Is he sick?"

"He's a little weak. Just cuddle with him and keep him company. Can you do that?"

Steffi ignored her question, but Genevieve jumped up and down. "I can. I can."

Coop tweaked one of Steffi's curls. "Be gentle with

him. I'm leaving Mrs. Fletcher our key so she can get your stuff for the sleepover. Daddy has some work to do."

Steffi's blue eyes rose from Buddy and flicked between Kendall and Coop. "Okay, Daddy."

Britt walked them to the door. "They'll be fine, but you're picking up Buddy before the party, right? I have a feeling some of the little girls don't like dogs as much as these two do."

"I just need to question someone, Britt. I won't be long."

Britt's eyes widened. "I hope this doesn't mean someone's going to start terrorizing pets again. We lost a cat the last time."

Coop squeezed her shoulder. "I think this one is personal. Thanks again."

On the way to Mrs. Binder's house, Kendall asked, "Do you really think Gary will be there? He could've hit the road already."

"If he has, maybe we can get something out of Raylene."

The truck rolled down the slick asphalt of a street that the Evergreen revival had bypassed. Weeds poked up from cracks in the sidewalk and water swirled around gutters clogged with leaves and debris.

"Baker Street is still an eyesore. Why doesn't the city council do something about the conditions here?"

"The mayor and his pal Jordan Young have bigger, more profitable fish to fry." Coop pulled in front of a gray, clapboard house with a sagging roof and a front yard choked by weeds. He pointed out the window. "Binder's bike."

"I didn't figure he'd hightail it out of Timberline on his ten-speed."

"Raylene's car is here, too, so if he left town he did it on foot."

Coop parked the truck and as Kendall's boots hit the ground, a curtain at the front window twitched. If Gary didn't want to talk to them, he wouldn't open the door.

They walked up the porch and Coop rapped on the crooked screen door. Several seconds later, the front door opened a crack.

"Yes?"

Coop cleared his throat. "Good afternoon, Mrs. Binder, is Gary home?"

"He's home but he's sick."

Kendall ground her back teeth together. "Can we talk to him for a minute?"

"Ma, is that Ms. Rush?" Gary's voice, weak and strained, filtered to the front porch.

Mrs. Binder looked over her shoulder. "And the sheriff."

"Let 'em in."

Gary's mother widened the door and stepped back.

Coop walked in first, as if shielding Kendall, but if he expected some kind of threat from Gary Binder, he'd misjudged the man. Had she?

Gary lay on the couch, huddled beneath a blanket, in front of a cooking show on TV. He muted the sound and struggled to sit up.

"I'm really sorry I didn't get much done today, ma'am. After I ate my lunch, I felt real sick. Too sick to even leave you a note. I did put all the tools away, and I have a receipt for a new line I had to buy for the weed whacker."

"D-did you see Buddy?" She put one hand on her hip.

"Buddy?"

"The dog."

"Oh, Gary don't like dogs." Mrs. Binder flapped her hands in the air. "Ever since he got bit once."

"Quiet, Ma." Gary swung his bare feet to the floor.

Raylene pulled her sweater around her skinny frame. "I'll be outside if you need me."

Gary rolled his eyes. "I didn't see the dog, ma'am. I didn't go out back today."

Coop's eyes met hers and he lifted his brows. "When Kendall and I got back to her place, she found Buddy lying on his side, sick. We took him to Doc Washburn, who said the dog had been poisoned."

"Poisoned?" Gary clutched the blanket around his middle. "I didn't poison no dog. Is that what you think? Is that why you're here?"

Coop took several more steps into the cluttered room and hovered over Gary still sitting on the couch. "That's what we thought. The dog was sick, you were gone."

Gary bounded from the couch and immediately grabbed the back, as he swayed on his feet. "I swear, Sheriff. I don't like dogs, but I wouldn't hurt one. I got sick. I got sick, too, maybe just like that dog."

Kendall folded her arms across her midsection. "What are you saying, Gary?"

He swiped the back of his hand across his mouth and sank to the arm of the couch. "Someone poisoned that dog…and someone poisoned me."

Chapter Fourteen

Coop stepped behind Kendall, who looked as unsteady as Gary. Narrowing his eyes, he studied the pale-faced ex-con. Was this guy on the level?

"Do you know any reason why someone would want to poison you along with a dog?"

Binder chewed on the side of his thumb. "Dunno."

"And yet that's the conclusion you jumped to?"

"Dog's sick, poisoned, and I get sick at the same time." Binder rubbed the back of his neck where he sported a tattoo of a star. "Could be poison. I don't have any insurance to see a doctor."

Kendall had regained her color and took a deep breath. "What did you eat for lunch?"

"A bologna sandwich on white bread and some potato chips. I had one of those chocolate cupcakes, but I didn't get to it. Upchucked everything."

Coop stuffed his hands in his pockets. "Did you say you left Kendall's house today before you got sick?"

"I had to get the lines for the weed whacker." He glanced at Kendall. "I have the receipt."

Coop's pulse picked up a beat. "Did you leave your lunch at the house when you went?"

"Yeah." Binder lurched forward. "And I didn't poison no dog, ma'am. I wouldn't do that."

"Do you know who would?" A muscle ticked at the corner of Coop's mouth.

Binder's eyes widened. "What? How would I know that?"

"Weren't you around these parts a few years ago when pets were turning up dead?"

The screen door banged and Raylene charged into the room reeking of tobacco. "My boy wouldn't hurt no animals. One of your guys questioned him about that and nothin' came of it."

"I believe you, Gary." Kendall put her hand on Gary's arm. "You should go get checked out by a doctor. Go see Dr. Crandall and I'll foot the bill."

Binder's face turned bright red. "That's okay, ma'am. I'm feeling better, and I can finish the job tomorrow."

"I insist. Get checked out before you come by tomorrow morning."

With further pressure from his mother, Binder agreed to make an appointment with Dr. Crandall.

When they got in the truck, Coop turned to her. "You want to find out if Binder was poisoned, right? That's the reason you were so adamant about his appointment with Dr. Crandall."

"I believe him, don't you?"

He started the truck and drove off of Baker Street. Once he turned the corner, he answered. "I can understand why someone might want to kill Buddy if that someone murdered Rawlings, not that we know yet what happened to Rawlings, but why risk killing Binder?"

"Binder's not dead."

"Because in his words, he upchucked everything."

She grimaced. "I just wish that security system was operational."

"You and me both. Every time I try to finish up, something gets in the way." He smacked the steering wheel. "I'm going to finish tonight."

"Since Steffi is at the sleepover, I'll make you dinner and we can both convalesce with Buddy." She stretched her arms over her head. "I feel like I've been run over by a semi today."

He touched the bandage on her cheek. "Someone tried to shoot you and someone poisoned your dog. Can't get much worse than that."

"Oh, I think it can get worse, especially if the person who shot at me and the person who poisoned Buddy is the same guy."

Coop let her suspicion hang in the air, not because he thought Kendall was off track, but because he had no answers for her.

If the present-day kidnapper of Harrison and Cheri was threatening Kendall, Coop may not know why but he'd do everything in his power to stop him and protect her...and this time he wouldn't need a psychologist to help him.

"How's the patient?" Coop peered around the edge of the screen door, wiping his boots on the mat outside.

Kendall patted the top of a sleeping Buddy's head, as his tail rose and fell in a halfhearted attempt at a wag. "He's fine. Is the security system operational?"

"It is." Leaning against the doorjamb, he pulled off

one boot and dropped it on the porch. "I'm going to leave my muddy boots out here. I don't want to spoil Annie's handiwork."

"Good idea, although Dreamweavers is coming back after the estate sale for a final cleanup." She lifted the computer from her lap. "Can you show me how to tap into my security cameras?"

"Let me wash up first." He lifted his nose and sniffed the air. "My stomach just growled. What's cookin'?"

"I have a pot roast in the oven with some potatoes. Do you want a salad with that or some green beans?"

"I'll take the green beans. Do you need any help?"

"Nope." She pointed to the hallway. "You get cleaned up and then show me how to access my security system. The dinner is cooking itself at this point."

He gave her a mock salute and sauntered toward the hallway in stocking feet.

Watching his rolling, rangy gait, she fanned herself. The man didn't even have to get cleaned up to look hot as hell.

How'd she get so lucky? Timberline's sheriff could've been old, potbellied Sheriff Carpenter who'd ruled over the town for most of her time here. Instead she'd gotten washboard abs, or at least she imagined Coop had washboard abs beneath his layers of clothing. Would she have a chance to find out before she left? Did she even want to know what she'd be missing?

Coop emerged from the hallway with his short hair slicked back, his flannel shirt tossed over one shoulder. "Ahh, that's better."

She narrowed her eyes, taking in the way his white

T-shirt clung to his muscles—including his six-pack. She hadn't been wrong.

He dangled the shirt from his fingertips. "I'm sorry. Did I get too comfortable? My shirt got wet outside."

"You did all the work. Get as comfortable as you like."

Her mouth watered as he dropped the flannel and stretched, his biceps bunching and the T-shirt clinging to his pecs. Police work in a small town must be more active than she thought.

He dropped beside her on the sofa and she dipped, her shoulder bumping his. "Okay, let's take a look."

He reached across her, and the soap in the bathroom had never smelled as good as it did on his warm skin. He tapped a few keys on the keyboard to bring up the security system. "You can also get this app on your phone."

He led her through the easy steps it took to view the video footage of her house and to check the alerts when they came through.

"You can turn this all over to the new owners when the time comes. Even if they choose to tear the place down and put up a mini mansion, they can reconnect the system."

She sank back against the cushion. "Even if they don't keep it, I feel so much better having it in place, especially after today."

Coop scratched Buddy behind the ear. "If I'd gotten it connected sooner, we would've seen exactly what happened to Buddy today...and Gary."

"Do you believe him?"

"If Gary did poison Buddy for some reason, he's not

the one who took a shot at you. Even if he'd taken his mother's car to Port Angeles, I don't think he would've had enough time to get there, set up, escape, come back here and feign an illness, even with Raylene's cooperation."

She shoved her computer from her lap to the cushion next to her. "What if the sniper was a general kook just looking to cause some mayhem? The shooting was all over the news. What if Gary thought he could make friends with Buddy by sharing some of his lunch with him, and that lunch was bad and made them both sick? When he realized what he'd fed Buddy made him sick, he panicked. Gary Binder is all about doing the right thing now."

"I'd like to believe all that, Kendall." He picked up a lock of her hair and twirled it around his finger.

"But you don't."

"That would require too many far-fetched coincidences."

"And in your line of work, you've come to suspect far-fetched coincidences?" She folded her hands in her lap and studied her fingernails. "I don't believe in coincidences, either. But you know what I do believe in?"

"What?" He released her hair and watched it spill against his hand.

"Fate."

"Fate, like destined by the stars or something?"

"Sort of." She took his hand and traced the pad of her thumb over his knuckles. "You saved my life today. You pushed me out of the way of that second shot. If you hadn't been with me, I'd be dead."

"Maybe if I hadn't dragged you into this investigation, you wouldn't have a target on your back." He clenched his hand into a fist beneath her touch.

"You don't really believe that, do you? That pink ribbon showed up in my aunt's cabinet before you ever knocked on my door. Someone was waiting for my return, for whatever reason." A chill skittered up her spine. "Maybe it's the same man who took my sister and kicked me into unconsciousness."

"Usually violent criminals don't stop their activity only to take it up twenty-five years later, unless..."

"Unless they've been in prison. You mentioned that before, but the thought of hapless Gary Binder as some vicious kidnapper is ludicrous."

"Haven't you ever watched the news stories after the capture of some serial killer? All his neighbors go on and on about what a nice guy he was—fixing bikes for the kids, taking in stray dogs—and at night he's going out and slashing hookers' throats."

She dug her fingernails into the back of his hand. "Ugh. Thanks for that visual."

The timer dinged from the kitchen. "That's dinner. Give me a shove so I can get up from this cushion. I don't even think I can sell this sofa."

Coop placed a firm hand on the small of her back, his fingers curling around her hip.

She sprang from the sofa, afraid she'd fall back into his arms where she wanted to be right now.

As she bounded toward the kitchen, Coop followed and hung on the doorjamb. "You know what I'd do if I bought this house?"

"Raze it to the ground?" She grabbed two oven mitts and gripped the handles of the roasting pan.

"I'd knock out the wall between the living room and kitchen, make it one big room with an island or peninsula counter separating the two areas."

"It is kind of old-fashioned having the solid wall between the two rooms and a doorway into the kitchen." The heat rose from the oven, warming her cheeks. She placed the roast on top of the stove and poked at the quartered potatoes in the pan. "Do these look done to you, or do you prefer them crispier?"

He broke off a corner of one potato with a fork and blew on it before popping it into his mouth. He rolled his eyes to the ceiling. "Perfect."

"I know my cooking's not *that* good."

"To a single dad, this is a piece of heaven right here." He waved his fork over the pot roast. "I can't do this. My cooking skills are basic."

"Then your skills are perfectly suited to cutting the green beans into two-inch pieces, washing them and sticking them in the microwave. Then you can toss them with a little lemon juice and parsley."

"Lead me to the green beans."

When they'd set the table and Coop had sliced pieces of meat from the pot roast, Kendall held up a bottle of red wine. "You're still officially on vacation, right?"

"One glass." Pinching the stem of the wineglass, he held it out to her and she poured the ruby-red liquid almost to the rim. "Whoa. You'd never make it as a sommelier."

"If they're stingy with their wine, then you're right."

She grabbed the back of her chair, but he got there first and pulled it out for her. "After the day you had, I don't know why you were in here cooking up a storm."

"Someone took a couple of shots at me and poisoned my dog." She jerked her shoulders up and down. "What am I supposed to do, assume the fetal position?"

He clinked his glass against hers. "I can never imagine you doing that. Even when you were five years old, you fought back."

She choked on her wine and pressed a napkin to her mouth. "What made you say that?"

"Your sister was sleeping and you kicked the kidnapper in the shins. She was taken. You weren't."

"I tried to save Kayla, too, not just myself." She took a bigger gulp of her wine, and her eyes watered.

"Kendall." Coop crossed his fork and knife on the edge of his plate. "You were five. Knowing you, I'm sure you did more than most five-year-olds would've done in that circumstance. You didn't curl up in a ball then, either."

She blinked. "That's why I became a therapist, you know. I try to save people a little bit every day."

"And I'm sure you do." He covered her hand with his.

She snatched her hand away and sawed into a piece of meat. "I'm not sure you have much faith in psychology."

"I have faith in you." He tapped her plate with his knife.

"I couldn't even protect *him*." She jerked her thumb over her shoulder at Buddy, sleeping in a basket in the corner. "That's why I've always avoided pets... and children."

"You did save Buddy. You checked on him, took him

straight to the vet, noticed the piece of poisoned sandwich meat and now he's recuperating nicely."

Coop had completely avoided her statement about kids. He had to realize by now she and he were completely wrong for each other, even though the air sizzled between them and his touch sent a thrill racing through her blood.

She stabbed a potato with her fork. "He does look pretty darned good, doesn't he?"

They managed to finish their meal without any more deep, dark confessions slipping from her lips. She'd never admitted to anyone except her therapist her reasons for studying psychology and going into private practice. Of course, that private practice didn't include children or families. She didn't think she could handle any failure in that area.

After Coop claimed the last potato, he tossed his napkin onto the table. "I'm going to wash all these dishes, and you're going to have another glass of wine and relax in the other room."

"You did your share of work on the security system today. Just leave the dishes. I'll deal with them tomorrow."

"No way." He started collecting the plates. "My mama taught me never to leave dirty dishes in the sink."

Kendall warmed her wineglass between her palms. "Did your mother come out here and help you? After...?"

"My mother, my sister and my aunt. I got a crash course in housekeeping, not that I was a slouch at it before. My wife...sometimes she couldn't even get out of bed in the morning."

"I'm sorry, Coop." She put her hand on his forearm, tracing the corded muscle with her fingertips.

The faraway look left his blue eyes and he smiled. "I do the best I can for Steffi, and we have a good life."

"You do a great job with your daughter. Don't beat yourself up." She rubbed a circle on his wrist. "Father of the Year."

"And now I'm bucking for Sheriff of the Year." He poured her another glass of wine. "Go. Unwind."

Her eyes met his over the rim of the glass as the fruity wine trickled down her throat. If she unwound any more, she'd end up in a puddle at his feet.

He swallowed and held up the plates. "Dishes."

She pivoted and returned to the living room where she dragged her computer onto her lap. "You do realize there's no TV in here?"

He called above the running water. "I noticed. Steffi wouldn't last five minutes in this house."

Kendall unzipped her boots and propped her feet on top of the coffee table while she accessed her new security system, courtesy of Sheriff of the Year. "All clear."

Coop's head appeared at the kitchen door. "What are you saying in there?"

"Go back to the dishes." She waved her hand.

By the time she'd reviewed every side of the house and the land in the back, Coop returned to the living room with a glass of water.

"Thanks for dinner. It was great. Are you feeling more relaxed now? You've checked your home security, Buddy's snoozing in the kitchen and you're on your second glass of wine."

She raised her half-empty glass. "And I have Timberline's vacationing sheriff by my side."

He took the glass from her and rubbed his thumb across the lipstick smudge on the rim, never losing eye contact with her. "And I'm staying right here."

Kendall swallowed. "Coop, I—I'm not your wife."

He swirled the wine in her glass where it caught the lamplight. "Not by a long shot."

"I mean," she said as she brushed her knuckles across the soft denim encasing his thighs, "I may need rescuing from time to time, but I don't need saving. Does that make sense?"

"Do you think I'm trying to save you?"

"I just don't want there to be any confusion about what this is between us."

"What is it?" He placed the wineglass on the coffee table and laced his fingers with hers.

A tingle of pleasure zigzagged through her body, and her eyelids fluttered as a small breath escaped her lips. "It's...it's not forever. I'm not staying here."

"I tried telling myself that." He kissed her fingertips, and then pressed her hand against his thundering heart. "And I don't need forever, do you? I just need right now."

Curling her fingers against the white cotton of his T-shirt, she whispered, "I'm glad you said it first."

Keeping her hand against his chest, Coop curled his other arm around her shoulders and brought her in for a kiss. His lips moved against hers tentatively as if questioning her commitment to the here and now.

She parted her lips and drew his tongue into her

mouth. She felt no hesitation about being with Coop and wanted him to know it.

He cupped the back of her head and deepened the kiss, sealing his mouth over hers. A longing so powerful washed over her, she jerked away from him to gasp for air.

His blue eyes glittered beneath half-mast eyelids as he tilted his head. "Is that a no?"

Even if she lived to regret this night, even if this man made all other men in her future pale by comparison, even if he invaded her dreams on hot, restless, Arizona nights, she couldn't put the brakes on her desire for his touch.

Entwining her arms around his neck, she breathed into his ear. "Yesss."

He buried one hand in her hair, tugging until her head tipped back. He pressed a kiss against the base of her throat, and her pulse throbbed beneath his lips. Or was that his pulse? She'd lost all sense of the boundaries between them.

She bunched his T-shirt in her hands and managed to get out one strangled word. "Bedroom."

He shot up as if on springs, taking her with him. Standing face-to-face, toe-to-toe, they stared into each other's eyes. They must've seen the same thing because she went willingly into his arms at the same time he pulled her closer.

Coop melded every line of his body against hers, and his kiss scorched her lips.

She wiggled away from him to reach beneath his T-shirt and skim her hands across the hard planes of his chest and flat belly. When she tweaked his nipple, he nipped her lip and she smiled beneath his kiss. She finished her exploration by hooking her fingers in the waistband of his jeans.

He sucked in a harsh breath. "I thought we were moving this party to the bedroom."

Sliding her fingers farther into his pants with one hand, she crooked the index finger of her other. "This way, Sheriff."

His stride matched hers but she kept her hold on him anyway, not willing to relinquish the warm feel of his skin against her fingertips.

When they got to the bedroom, he walked her backward to the bed until the back of her knees pressed against the mattress. Wasting no time, he grabbed the bottom of her sweater and pulled it over her head.

He sighed as he ran a finger from the neckline of her camisole to where she'd tucked it into her jeans. "You're wearing too many layers."

"I can fix that." She tugged the camisole out of her pants, but she must've been moving too slowly to satisfy him, because he snatched the thin cotton from her fingers and yanked off the camisole and tossed it over his shoulder.

Hooking his fingers around the straps of her bra, he said, "This better be it."

She giggled like a high school girl in the backseat of the star football player's muscle car.

And with probably as much practice as that star football player, Coop unhooked her bra in the back. He then planted a trail of kisses from her jaw to her shoulder and pulled at the bra strap with his teeth.

With a little cooperation and a lot of impatience from her, the lacy bra fell to the floor.

He cradled her breasts in his large hands, his thumbs toying with her nipples, which peaked and ached beneath his touch. Standing on her tiptoes, she nibbled his ear and flicked his lobe with her tongue.

Craving the full skin-to-skin contact, she lifted his T-shirt. "Talk about layers. Take this off."

He complied and in a nanosecond he had her back in his arms. When chest met chest, bare skin against bare skin, Kendall hissed just to provide the sound effect for their connection—and they had a connection. She could almost see the steam rising from their bodies.

"You feel so good." Coop's ragged voice had her digging her nails into his back to urge him on.

This might just be a one-nighter, but at least it wasn't going to be a quickie. If this was going to be the first, last and only time they indulged their desire, she needed an overdose of Coop to keep her going through those long, lonely nights in Phoenix.

As if sensing her urgency, Coop stripped out of his jeans and boxers with lightning speed. Fully naked, he nudged her onto the bed and, straddling her hips, he pulled her jeans, panties and socks from her in one continuous motion.

He hovered above her and traced a slow line from her chin to her mound with the tip of his finger while she squirmed beneath him. He flashed a grin that would do the devil proud. "Don't be so impatient. I need lots of memories to get me through the cold, rainy nights ahead."

She whispered, trying to keep the sob from her voice, "I was just thinking the same thing."

"Then let's make some memories."

He lowered himself on top of her, his erection throbbing against her thigh. Her skin, flushed with warmth, tingled from the tips of her toes to the top of her head… and everywhere in between.

Stroking her palms across the hard muscle of his buttocks, she hooked one leg around his calf. She wanted him inside her now, but she was willing to humor him and go along with the buildup.

His lips found the nipple of her left breast, and he teased her by sucking on it and then blowing against her moist skin, and all of a sudden, the buildup didn't seem like such a bad idea.

As she explored his body with her hands, he made love to every part of hers with his lips, his tongue, his teeth, setting her nerve endings on fire. When he brought her to climax, it took him just a few flicks of his tongue to send her over the edge.

He entered her as she was still descending from the precipice of her release. She pressed her lips against his collarbone to keep her scream in check as he drove into her.

Sensing her reserve, Coop growled in her ear. "Why are you holding back? Give it to me."

Her head fell to the side and she released a slow moan that had started somewhere in her tummy. As the friction and excitement built up between them, she wrapped her legs around his pumping hips, clamping around him as if she was riding a mechanical bull—

but there was nothing mechanical about this bull. Coop was all hot flesh and hotter kisses.

She started to unravel beneath him, the tight coil in her belly spinning out of control. As her second climax scooped her up onto another wave of desire, Coop shuddered and groaned, a deep guttural sound.

His eyes had been closed, but now his eyelids flew open and he pinned her with a deep blue gaze as he came inside her. She tried focusing on his orgasm, she tried focusing on her own, and then gave up and went along for the delicious ride.

When they were both spent, Coop rolled onto his back and draped one heavy leg over hers. "I knew that was gonna be good."

"Mmm, I had the same suspicion, but you exceeded my expectations."

"I wanted to commit every bit of you to memory." He entwined his fingers with her. "Just in case we don't get another opportunity before you leave."

Her nose stung and she rubbed the tip of it. "You're going to be a busy man once your vacation is over."

A muffled buzzing noise came from the floor at the foot of the bed.

She pinched Coop's thigh. "That must be your phone because mine's in the other room."

He winked at her and scrambled toward the foot of the bed, leaned over and rustled through his jeans. "Got it."

Sitting up, she drew her knees to her chest, a feather of fear drifting across the back of her neck. "Is it the station?"

"No." He drew his brows over his nose as he

squinted at the display. "It's Britt. I hope Steffi hasn't gotten sick stuffing herself on popcorn, brownies and soda.

"Hey, Britt, everything okay?"

Kendall clutched the sheet to her chest as all color drained from Coop's face. Everything wasn't okay— not at all.

"Coop? What's wrong?"

His eyes met hers and she flinched at the ferocity in their blue depths.

"He has Steffi."

Chapter Fifteen

Blackness engulfed him from all sides. He couldn't hear Kendall's words even though her mouth was moving and he could no longer hear Britt's wailing over the roaring in his ears.

He couldn't have her. He couldn't have his little girl.

Dropping the phone, he launched from the bed and dragged on his jeans.

Kendall was beside him in an instant, her hand on his arm. "I'll drive you."

His gaze swept over her naked body, still dewy from their lovemaking, and he blinked. That seemed light-years away now.

How could he have let Steffi down like this? He should've never let her out of his sight.

Three children. A trio of children. The Timberline Trio. Two girls and one boy. He should've known the kidnapper would strike again.

Following his gaze, Kendall's cheeks flamed, as if realizing for the first time she was naked, as if he hadn't already explored every intimate detail of her body.

Reaching behind her, she dragged the sheet off the

bed and draped it around her shoulders. "Give me a minute to get dressed. You shouldn't be driving."

What did she see? He jerked his head toward the mirror above the dresser. Except for his heaving chest, he didn't look like a man who had just lost everything in the world.

His hands curled into fists and every muscle in his body coiled into a hard spring. He would do some serious damage to the piece of garbage who'd snatched Steffi—once he got his hands on him. *If* he got his hands on him.

Kendall, now fully dressed, shoved his T-shirt against his chest. "Finish dressing and let's get going. The faster you get all the details, the faster we'll get Steffi back."

He stared at the shirt in his hands as if he'd forgotten what to do with it. "We didn't get Kayla back, did we? Or Harrison? Or Cheri?"

"Stop." She gripped both of his wrists, digging her nails into his flesh. "We're getting her back—all of them. This guy just made a colossal mistake."

He finished dressing, his body ping-ponging back and forth between fright and flight. One moment he felt overwhelmed and close to panic and the next he wanted to smash something…or somebody.

Kendall brought him back to earth, shoving a plastic bottle under his nose. "Have some water and give me your keys."

He dug into his pocket and dragged out his keys. He dropped them into her outstretched palm, her wiggling fingers the only sign of agitation.

She led the way to the truck and climbed behind the wheel.

Putting a hand over hers as she inserted the key in the ignition, he said, "Are you sure you're okay to drive after drinking that wine?"

"I had two glasses, it was a while ago and I...uh... engaged in some physical activity. I'll be fine."

He directed her back to the Fletchers' place where two cruisers were already parked out front, their lights spinning and casting an eerie glow on a nightmarish tableau of parents frantically hugging their crying children and dragging them away from the scene of the crime.

Britt stopped sobbing long enough to rush toward him, babbling apologies and explanations.

Coop enfolded her in a hug. He couldn't blame her. He was at fault. He should've been watching over Steffi instead of...

"Coop, come on inside and I'll give you what we have." Sergeant Payton pulled him away from Britt's death grip. "Agent Maxfield is on the way with the rest of the task force."

"They've had almost a month to find the other two children. I don't have a lot of faith in him or his band of pencil pushers." Reaching back, he grabbed Kendall's hand. She was the only thing keeping him sane right now. "Come with us, Kendall. I need you."

As she trailed after him and Payton to the house, she squeezed his hand. Amid the chaos, he heard her whisper, "I'm here."

When they entered the house, Rob led them to the den and closed the door. "My wife's hysterical. I think it's better that she stay with her sister right now. She's not going to be much use."

Coop paced the room, plowing a hand through his hair. "Britt said the girls were outside. My God, Rob, what were five-year-old girls doing outside?"

Rob covered his face. "They snuck out, just Genevieve, Molly and Steffi. From what we could get out of Genevieve, someone threw pebbles at the window. They thought—" he choked "—they thought it was a wood sprite, like that movie about the fairies and elves. *The Fairies of the Glen.* They're obsessed with that damned movie."

Coop crossed his arms, hunching his shoulders. He knew that movie well. Did the kidnapper know it, too? He had to know how appealing that gesture would've been to a bunch of little girls. But why *his* little girl? Was it just a coincidence, or had he been aiming for the sheriff's daughter?

Payton cleared his throat. "You didn't hear the girls coming downstairs or going out the back door?"

"Britt and I were in the bedroom with the door shut." Rob reddened to the roots of his thinning hair. "We should've left the door open. We were going to check on the girls later, but all seemed quiet at the time."

Judging by his blush, Rob and Britt were probably engaged in the same activity as he and Kendall.

"How are the other girls?" Coop massaged the back of his neck.

"Upset, traumatized." Rob broke into a sob and Kendall covered her eyes with one hand.

God, this had to be hard for her, too—reliving this nightmare she thought she'd escaped.

Coop swallowed. "Did the girls see anything?"

"It was dark. As they crept closer to the edge of the woods, a man, masked, all in black materialized."

Kendall gasped.

"Without saying a word, he snatched Steffi. The girls ran screaming into the house."

A tap on the door broke the tension in the room. "Agent Maxfield here."

Coop rolled his eyes at Payton. "Let him in."

The sergeant got up from behind the desk and opened the door.

The agent charged into the room like he owned it, his minions following closely on his heels. "Sheriff, I'm sorry about your daughter. We're going to nail this SOB. What do we have so far?"

Rob went through his story again and Payton chimed in about the search they were conducting in back of the house.

"I saw the spotlights out there. Good job, Sergeant, but we brought in our own equipment and we'll take it from here."

The agents continued talking about a whole lotta nothing until Coop stopped his pacing and strode to the door. "Less talking and more doing. I want to see where Steffi was snatched. If that bastard left one thread, I'm going to find it and hunt him down."

Payton couldn't do anything but follow him outside, and Rob went to console his wife and the children.

Coop didn't have a wife or a child to console.

He turned to Kendall, still by his side. "You can stay in the house if you like."

She shook her head. "I need the fresh air."

Law enforcement personnel milled around outside along with anxious parents, who had come back after securing their children at home.

Coop led the way around the back of the house and looked up at the window of the room where the girls had been giggling, watching movies and eating popcorn. Hadn't he taught Steffi better? How many more times could he fail his family?

His officers had collected several small rocks on the ground that the kidnapper could've used to pelt the window. But if the guy was wearing gloves, they'd get no prints. Any shoe prints looked like they'd been smoothed over and there were more scuff marks than solid prints.

Coop continued to stare at the ground until his eyes ached, but despite the FBI crowing over an old cigarette butt and a few freshly snapped twigs, nothing of substance materialized.

He rubbed his eyes and looked up, studying the faces of the local crowd that had gathered around the newest focal point of tragedy.

He peered into the darkness, straining his eyes, looking for Kendall. But she was gone, too.

Would everyone of importance in his life disappear?

KENDALL STARED AT the text glowing in the dark.

Do you want another chance, Kendal? Do you want to save Kayla? Walk to the wooded path behind the new house. Come alone and dont say a word or they all die.

He didn't spell her name right and didn't know how to use contractions, but the meaning was clear.

With her heart doing somersaults in her chest, Kendall looked up from her phone. Knots of people huddled together discussing this newest development. Coop was still in the back with the FBI agents and Sergeant Payton.

Nobody was watching her. Could she do this? Could she make a difference? Could she save Coop's daughter?

The kidnapper had wanted to involve her all along. Maybe it was the same man from twenty-five years ago, maybe not, but she had a chance here.

She'd given Coop the keys to his truck after she'd parked it. Should she chance leaving him a note on the windshield? She scanned the crowd of looky-loos. Was the kidnapper watching her now? She couldn't chance leaving a note for Coop—too much at stake.

Looking both ways, she scurried down the wet sidewalk recently installed in front of this new development of homes. As she made her way to the new house, the only one yet to sell, she replied to the text message but it bounced back. He'd blocked her number.

The noise and lights in front of the Fletchers' house faded as the dark night enclosed around her. She picked her way across the unlandscaped front lawn and headed to the woods behind the house.

Realtors like Rebecca used that stretch of forest behind these houses as a selling point, but they might have to rethink their strategy after this night.

Her boots stuck in the mud and she had to pull them

free with each step. She called out with one breathless word. "Hello?"

Her muscles froze. Was that a twig snapping?

She edged closer to the tree line, walking on the balls of her feet, adrenaline coursing through her veins.

A whoosh of air at her back had her making a half turn, but it was too late. The rough cloth, soaked with chloroform closed over her nose and mouth. She shoved her tongue against the gag. She twisted in her captor's grip. She reached behind her to claw at him. But none of it did any good.

And the night got darker.

Chapter Sixteen

A sticky finger prodded her cheek. "Wake up."

Kendall squeezed her eyes shut, trying to wring out the pain throbbing against her temples. She peeled her tongue from the roof of her dry mouth and ran it across her teeth.

"Open your eyes." Her tormentor poked her in the back. "You need to wake up."

Kendall moaned and rolled onto her back. A sweet taste lingered in her mouth and she tried to spit it out, but her mouth was like a desert. A wisp of hair tickled her cheek and she focused on moving her hand to brush it away.

Drugged. She felt drugged, groggy.

A jolt of fear zapped her body and her eyelids clicked open like a doll's. Chloroform. Someone had drugged her, incapacitated her with chloroform.

A heart-shaped face curtained by long, blond ringlets hovered over her. "Finally."

"Steffi?" Kendall struggled to sit up. Was this a dream? Small hands pulled at her arms, and her head fell to the side.

A dark-haired boy tugged on her arm again. "Are you okay?"

A sob bubbled up in her throat and she choked. "Harrison? Are you Harrison Keaton?"

He cocked his head, his dirty, stringy hair brushing his shoulder. "Uh-huh. How'd you know that?"

Steffi, kneeling beside Kendall, put a hand on her hip. "Everyone knows you, Harrison. You're kidnapped."

Blinking her eyes to focus in the dark, Kendall dragged herself to a sitting position and leaned against one rough stone wall of their prison. "Cheri? Is Cheri here?"

"She's sleeping." Steffi pointed to a dark form curled up on a straw mat.

Kendall spread out her arms and enfolded both children into a giant bear hug. "Oh, my God. I am so happy to see all of you. Are you all right?"

"I'm hungry." Harrison kicked at a crumpled, white bag. "All he ever gives us is fast food. My mom's says I'm not allowed to eat fast food."

"I hope you've been eating, Harrison." Kendall rubbed her thumb across a smudge on the boy's dirty face. You've been missing for almost a month. Have you been here the whole time?"

"I dunno." He shrugged his shoulders.

Kendall looked around, running her hand across the rock at her back. "Where is here? It looks like we're in some kind of cave. Steffi, were you awake when he brought you here?"

"No." She rubbed a hand across her lips. "He put stuff on my mouth and I went to sleep."

"Did you see him? Did you see his face?"

Steffi shook her head. "He had a mask on and gloves."

Harrison chimed in. "He always does. When he brings food and stuff. I can't see him."

"Where's the entrance?" Kendall staggered to her feet, tipping her head back.

"It's up there." Harrison pointed to the ceiling of the cave, which looked like an abandoned mine, clearly left over from Timberline's silver mining days.

She found a foothold in the cave wall and hoisted herself up to get a clearer view of the entrance. "Have you tried climbing up here?"

"I have." Harrison punched the wall with a small fist. "But there's a door or something blocking everything."

Kendall squinted into the gloom. No light appeared from the area at the top of the mine. Had he rolled a boulder over the entrance?

She hopped back to the ground, her gaze tracking over the two children in front of her—Steffi surprisingly calm after her ordeal and Harrison matter-of-fact and filthy.

Putting a hand on Harrison's shoulder, she asked, "Does he ever come down here? Does he ever talk to you or…touch you?"

The boy shook his head, his scraggly hair whipping across his face. "He never comes down here. Probably afraid of my ninja skills."

"Probably." Kendall smiled but drew her brows over her nose at the same time. What did he want? Was he involved in some kind of child trafficking and just waiting for his contact? Had he been waiting for an opportunity to snatch a third child?

And what did he want with *her*? Could it really be the same man who'd kidnapped Kayla all those years ago?

Steffi sniffled. "Kendall?"

"Yes, sweetie?" She ruffled the girl's baby-soft hair.

"Is my daddy going to find us?"

Kendall swallowed the lump in her throat. "Maybe. There sure are a lot of people looking for you right now."

A big tear rolled down Steffi's face. "I don't want to be here. It's dark. What if it rains?"

"It rains all the time." Harrison scuffed the toe of his shoe against the dirt. "Big deal."

"Does it come in here? Does the rain fill up the cave?" Steffi's eyes grew big and round, fear shining from their depths.

The tone of Steffi's voice clearly rattling him, Harrison peered at the ceiling. "I—I don't think so."

Steffi started to shake, and Kendall put an arm around her and led her back to the cave wall. She crouched down and straightened out a beach towel on the ground. "Let's sit down. Harrison, you too."

Kendall sank to the ground, shrugging off her jacket. She patted the towel next to her. "Sit, Steffi. Harrison, are you cold?"

"Nah." He plopped down next to her while Steffi lowered herself on Kendall's other side.

She wrapped her jacket around Steffi's trembling form and pulled her close. Steffi dropped her head on Kendall's shoulder.

"I wanna go home."

"I know, sweetie. When the man comes back, I'll talk to him. I'll find out what he wants us to do to get out of here."

The sleeping girl mumbled and sat up, rubbing her eyes. She yelped when she spotted Kendall.

"Cheri?"

She pressed herself against the wall of the cave and started crying.

Kendall's heart broke in two. She gestured with her hand. "Come on over here, Cheri. I'm Kendall. I'm not going to hurt you. We're going to keep warm together."

Harrison said to Cheri, "She was kidnapped, too, and she's gonna get us out."

Kendall bit her lip. Had she been kidnapped? What did her abductor have in store for her? Did he want to tie up the loose end that he'd left twenty-five years ago?

And could she get the children out?

Cheri crawled toward her, dragging a towel behind her.

"Are you okay, Cheri? You're not hurt, are you?"

She shoved her finger in her mouth, a regressive gesture for a six-year-old. Then she curled up next to Kendall and rested her head in her lap.

"Now that we're all together, do you want to play a game?"

"Ninja warriors?" Harrison looked up hopefully.

Kendall tugged on his ear. "How about I Spy?"

Steffi hiccupped through her tears. "It's dark. We can't spy anything."

"This is going to be imaginary I spy. You're going

to tell me what you *think* you see in the dark and we can turn this cave into anyplace you want."

Cheri popped her thumb from her mouth. "The fairies in the glen?"

"Not the fairies in the glen." Steffi's bottom lip trembled. "That's for babies."

Harrison started first, his voice echoing in the cave. "I spy a green dragon."

They all took turns, filling the cave with animals—real and mythical, cupcakes, swimming pools, one particular boy band and lots of food.

Kendall giggled so much, her sides hurt, and at the end of the game, Harrison yawned and said, "I'm glad you were kidnapped, too, Kendall."

"Me, too." Cheri burrowed her head against Kendall's lap.

And then Steffi whispered, "Me, too, Kendall."

As the children fell asleep around her, Kendall's mind raced. Maybe her nemesis from twenty-five years ago had done all this for her. Maybe he'd wanted her all along. He'd taken the wrong twin. Would he take her and leave the children? He hadn't harmed them...yet.

She brushed Harrison's cheek with her thumb and smoothed Steffi's hair back from her forehead. He wouldn't harm them as long as she stood guard over them. She'd give her life to protect these children, Coop's daughter.

And maybe that's what this pig wanted.

Coop banged on Kendall's door and Buddy whimpered and scratched at the wood inside. "Kendall?"

Stooping forward, he cupped his hand on the window and peeked through a gap in the drapes. Buddy jumped on the window, his claws scrabbling at the glass.

The squeak of a wheel had Coop spinning around and his gaze clashed with Binder's, as the ex-con rode up on his bike.

"Have you seen Kendall?"

"Just got here." Binder leaned his bike against a tree and scratched his beard. "I heard about your little girl, Sheriff. I'm sorry."

Coop narrowed his eyes and the man started fidgeting. "Did you ever go to the doctor?"

"Nope." He pulled the bill of his cap lower over his eyes. "My ma made me some soup and I drunk a bunch of sports drinks. I feel okay now. I wanna finish the job I started yesterday."

"Kendall's not home."

"I can still work. I got the tools around back."

Where had Kendall gone last night? She'd left his truck at the Fletchers'. Did she walk home? Catch a ride with someone there?

He'd taken a quick look for her before following Agent Maxfield to the task force war room and had tried calling her later, but her phone had been turned off. Was it time to triangulate that cell or was he overreacting?

He waited for Binder to come to the front of the house, lugging his gardening tools. Then Coop slipped around to the back, made a sharp tap on the window of the kitchen door to break it and let himself into Kendall's house. At least she had a security system to tell her who'd broken into her place.

Hearing his entry, Buddy ran into the kitchen, his paws skidding across the linoleum until he crashed into his ankles. "Easy, Buddy. Where's your mistress?"

He tucked the dog under one arm as he surveyed the kitchen. The dishes he'd washed last night after dinner were still stacked in the dish drainer on the counter. No coffee had been made, no breakfast dishes were piled in the sink.

Buddy whimpered, so he set him down. The dog trotted to his empty water dish and Coop's heart stuttered. No way would Kendall leave Buddy without any water.

He barreled into the living room, taking in the empty wineglass from last night sitting on the coffee table. He continued onto the bedroom. He pounded on the doorjamb when he saw the tousled covers of Kendall's bed—just the way they'd left them after making love.

Why hadn't she come home? Where was she? His mind wouldn't work. He'd been up all night scouring the area for Steffi, leading a search team, just as they'd done for the other two children—with the same results.

In a state of numbness, he let Buddy out into the backyard and filled his dishes with fresh water and some puppy kibble. He called Agent Maxfield to check for any updates and let him know that Kendall Rush seemed to be missing.

"Any signs of foul play?"

Coop's gaze darted around the living room, exactly the way they'd left it last night. "I can't tell, but she hasn't been home."

"She's an attractive woman. Maybe she has a boyfriend in town."

"She…" Coop snapped his mouth shut. What was the point? "Any other news?"

"We'll let you know as soon as we have something. We're doing our best, Sheriff."

Coop ended the call and shoved the phone into his pocket. The FBI's best wasn't good enough.

He secured Buddy in his pen on the back patio since he had no idea when Kendall would be coming back. Where could she have gone and why wasn't she returning his calls?

Memories of the shots ringing out in Port Angeles yesterday caused him to clench his jaw, already aching with tension and fear. Had Kendall gone looking for Steffi herself and gotten into trouble?

If the trouble included a run-of-the-mill car accident or sprained ankle in the woods, he would've heard something by now. Did the battery on her phone die because she hadn't been home to charge it? Had she turned it off to save it? Or was there a more sinister reason why her phone was offline?

He chucked Buddy under the chin. "Don't worry, pooch. I'll make sure you have water and food."

Rising from the ground, Coop brushed off the knees of his jeans and strode to the front of the house.

Binder had stopped working and was leaning against that rickety old bike of his, hands open in front of him, a water bottle on the ground at his feet.

His head jerked up at Coop's approach, his eyes wide in his gaunt face. He spun toward his bike and buried his hands in the saddlebag strapped to the handlebars of the bike.

Coop had been a cop long enough to recognize suspicious behavior, and he changed direction in midstride. "Whatcha got there, Binder?"

"Nothin'." Stooping over, he plucked his water bottle from the ground. "Just getting my water."

"What did you have in your hands?"

Binder peered at his empty hand as if it belonged to someone else. "Nothin'."

"Didn't you just put something in your satchel?"

"No." Binder grabbed the handlebars of his bike, the water bottle falling from his hand.

Coop launched forward and pushed Binder away from the bike. He flipped back the lid on the satchel and plunged his hands inside. His fingers curled around all of the items he could grab, and he yanked them out of the bag.

He opened his hands. His breath hitched in his throat as the plastic dinosaur tottered in his palm and the pink ribbon fluttered in the breeze.

"I—I didn't... I—I don't know." Binder put his hands in front of him in a defensive position.

Coop dropped the items, so indelibly linked to the kidnappings, and drew his fist back to smash into Binder's sickly face.

Chapter Seventeen

Kendall rubbed her eyes and shivered. She cuddled the kids closer to her body. How had these poor babies been keeping warm with just beach towels to cover them?

At least Wyatt and Cheri had been kidnapped wearing their jackets. Steffi just had her pink, flannel pajamas to protect her from the elements.

Kendall pulled her jacket more tightly beneath Steffi's chin and rubbed her arms.

Had Coop figured out yet that she'd gone missing? He was probably much too concerned about his daughter and not some woman he'd been having a one-night stand with when Steffi had been kidnapped. Was he blaming himself?

She should've texted him, left him a note on his truck, but she'd been afraid the kidnapper would see her and harm the children.

She sucked in her bottom lip and closed her eyes. What kind of therapist was she? She couldn't even be honest with herself. She'd wanted to save Steffi for Coop. She'd wanted to save all of the kids for herself, to make herself feel better after failing to protect Kayla.

When she opened her eyes, her gaze clashed with Steffi's. "You're awake."

"I'm not afraid, anymore." Steffi blinked her blue eyes, so like her father's. "I'm not afraid 'cuz you're here and it's daytime. My daddy will find us during the day, won't he?"

"It'll be easier during the daylight hours." She gestured around the mine. "This place can't be too far from town, from the road. He must've carried me here."

Harrison mumbled. "I'm hungry."

Kendall surveyed the little nest the children had cobbled together. "Does he leave you any extra food?"

"We had cereal and granola bars." Harrison yawned. "But those are gone."

"Maybe he'll bring us some food this morning, and I can talk to him." She had every intention of bargaining with this monster to free the children. The kids couldn't harm him. They hadn't seen him or heard him talk.

A scraping noise echoed from above, and Harrison grabbed her arm. "It's him."

"Cheri, wake up." She shook the little girl, who rolled over, instantly awake.

Kendall staggered to her feet, her head tilted back. "Hey! Hey, you! Let us out of here."

"Kendall? Kendall, is that you?" There was more scraping and a shaft of light skewered the floor.

Relief washed over her, and she braced a hand against the rock as her knees wobbled. "Wyatt?"

"Oh, my God, Kendall. What are you doing down there? Are those kids down there, too?"

Cheri started crying, Steffi stood up, clutching Kendall's hand and Harrison jumped up and down beside her. "I'm here! I'm here!"

"Yes. We're all here, Wyatt. Me, Harrison, Cheri and Steffi."

"Thank God I found you." He grunted and released a breath. "I can't move this boulder. I need some help."

"Oh, God. Please don't leave us here, Wyatt. He might come back."

"Who? Who put you here?"

"I have no idea. I didn't see him. The kids didn't see him." She put her arm around Cheri. "Please don't go away."

"I'm not going anywhere. I have cell phone reception out here. I'm going to call 9-1-1 and get some help moving this rock."

"Make sure they call the FBI and Coop. Please call Coop."

"I'm just going to step away where I can make the call. Hang on. It's gonna be okay."

Kendall made the kids come in for a group hug and Harrison chattered about all things he was going to do when he got out.

Wyatt interrupted their celebration. "I made the call. They're on their way. I can't really see you through the space. Is everyone okay?"

"The kids are fine. Everyone's fine." She wiped a tear from her face. "How'd you find us?"

"I saw something last night but it was too dark. Came back this morning."

Before he could go any further into detail, sirens called out in the distance and Kendall had never heard such a lovely sound.

Within minutes, even though it had seemed longer, the first responders above had rolled the rock from the opening and light flooded the cave.

The rescue began in earnest. The cheers Kendall heard above as each child was released warmed her heart and brought a big smile to her face. She was the last to come up and before the fireman could even unbuckle her from the harness, Coop had his arms around her.

"I was so worried about you." He kissed the side of her head. "Thank you. Thank you."

She pointed to Wyatt, surrounded by members of the FBI task force. "You should be thanking Wyatt."

"I did, believe me, but Steffi told me how you kept it all together down there, how you made them all feel better, not so scared."

Through misty eyes she watched Harrison and Cheri in their parents' arms, holding on like they'd never let go again. Then her gaze shifted to Steffi, sitting on the back of the ambulance. Their eyes met and Steffi waved.

"They're all incredible kids—brave, strong, fearless."

When the harness dropped from her body, Coop curled his arm around her neck and pulled her close. "You did it, Kendall. You made Kayla proud today."

As the FBI ushered Wyatt out of the forest, he turned to Kendall and gave her a thumbs-up. "Wyatt made Stevie proud, too."

A FEW DAYS LATER, Kendall boxed some of Aunt Cass's items that didn't sell during the daylong estate sale.

Wyatt had come late and was perusing a table littered with books and old record albums.

"You can help yourself, Wyatt."

"I'll pay. I wouldn't feel right otherwise."

"C'mon, you're the man of the hour. The mayor is going to declare Wyatt Carson day and give you the keys to the city."

He snorted, but his cheeks reddened with pleasure.

Coop pulled up in his truck and poked his head out the window. "Do you want me to haul the rest of this stuff to a donation center?"

Wyatt waved at Coop and then winked at Kendall. "I'll take this box in the house for you. Is Buddy still penned up in the back?"

"Yes." She turned away and rolled her eyes. How two grown men could be so afraid of a little dog, she'd never get.

Her heart skipped a beat, and she pressed her hand to her chest. But then one of those men may have had reason to fear Buddy.

Coop hopped from the truck and swooped in for a kiss. "How'd it go today?"

"Sold a lot of stuff." She spread her arms wide. "Even most of the furniture."

"Maybe the house isn't cursed anymore."

She shoved her fingers into her back pockets, palms outward. "Does the FBI really believe Gary Binder had something to do with the Timberline Trio kidnappings, too?"

"Maybe, but they still don't have enough evidence to tie him to the current ones. Raylene is giving him alibi after alibi."

"She would, right?" Kendall hunched her shoulders. She was torn between wanting to believe Gary was the kidnapper so the community could feel safe again, and disbelieving the polite, obsequious ex-con could've pulled it off.

"I think Raylene would do anything to protect her boy, even though her boy is a forty-five-year-old man with a past." He hugged her close and mumbled into her hair. "I can't wait to get out to Phoenix to see you."

"I can't wait, either." She curled her arms around his waist. "Even if Phoenix PD isn't hiring, there are other departments and agencies."

"I'm not worried. I'll find something." He jerked his thumb over his shoulder. "Do you want me to help you box up the rest of this stuff?"

"I'm good. Wyatt can help after he finishes picking through the leftovers." She smacked his behind. "Besides, you have to get back to work. Vacation over, Sheriff."

"Yeah, and what a vacation." He nibbled her ear. "Can you smack my backside again? It kind of turned me on."

She giggled. "We'll continue this in Phoenix."

"Can't wait." He pressed a kiss against her lips. "And don't forget. Dinner with me and Steffi tonight before I take you to the airport tomorrow morning, and don't forget to bring Buddy. We'll take care of him until we can reunite the two of you in Phoenix."

"I won't forget Buddy. How's Steffi doing?"

"She's fine. Having you there spared her an even greater trauma. You helped all the kids, and even Harrison and Cheri seem to be recovering. Harrison's parents are taking him to Disneyland, and Cheri's mom is taking her to Seattle to visit family."

"I'm glad. Now get back to work, so you can afford my dinner tonight."

They kissed again, long and lingering, since it would be their last time together alone until he dropped her off at the airport.

He held his hand out the window of the truck as he pulled out, and she blew him a kiss.

When Coop's truck disappeared, Kendall gathered up the remaining odds and ends from the estate sale and put them in two boxes. She carried the first one into the house, and Wyatt dropped an album cover he'd been studying to hold the screen door open for her.

"There's one more if you wouldn't mind bringing that in."

"Sure." He jogged down the steps and returned with the box in his arms, whistling a tune. "On the floor?"

"Yeah." She scrunched up her nose. "What's that song you're whistling? It's catchy."

"It's from that popular kids' movie, something about fairies."

A little chill touched her heart. That had been Steffi's favorite movie. "I didn't peg you as a fan of kids' animated films."

He chuckled. "I was doing a plumbing job for the Kendrick family and those kids must've watched that DVD twenty times while I was there."

She rubbed the gooseflesh on her arms. "If you want to take this box, you can, or I can have Rebecca Geist, my Realtor, drop it off for me tomorrow at a donation center."

"You're flying out tomorrow morning?"

"Yep. Back to Phoenix." She pointed to the box he'd been going through, anxious for him to be on his way so she could finish packing, get ready for dinner and most of all bring poor Buddy inside. "You can just take it all, Wyatt. Whatever you don't want, you can donate or sell at your next yard sale."

"I wouldn't feel right just taking it for free."

She patted him on the back. "You deserve it—hero."

He ducked his head. "I did it for Stevie. It felt good. You know, like we'd come full circle."

"Yeah, it did." Her nose stung and she sniffled.

"I'll tell you what." He pulled his wallet from his pocket by the chain attached to his belt. "I'll give you twenty bucks for the whole box."

"If you insist." She walked into the kitchen to wash her hands, and Wyatt followed her, peering into his wallet.

"Personal check okay? I only have a few bucks."

"Whatever you want to do, Wyatt." She probably wouldn't cash it anyway. She tugged a dish towel from the handle on the oven door and wiped her hands as Wyatt wrote out a check on the counter.

"Here you go." He slid the check across to her.

"Buddy, settle down." When they'd walked into the kitchen, the little dog had gone nuts, yapping and jumping against the wire mesh of his pen. "Sorry."

Wyatt shrugged, but his hand trembled when he put down the pen.

With one finger, she scooted the check toward her and glanced down at it. "Oh, you spelled my name…"

She froze.

He'd made it out to Kendal Rush. She stared at the spelling of her name. Kendall with one *l*, just like the text from the kidnapper—the text the FBI couldn't trace, the text they were having a hard time tying to Gary because Gary didn't own a cell phone and so far they'd turned up no records that he'd bought one.

The words on the check blurred in front of her eyes. *The Fairies of the Glen* was a new movie out in theaters. The kids couldn't be watching that movie on a DVD at home.

Wyatt made a small noise in the back of his throat.

Slowly, she raised her eyes to his, pasting a fake smile on her face. "Okay, well, thanks for the check and…everything."

He shook his head. "It won't do, Kendall. It won't do at all."

Chapter Eighteen

"Buckle your seat belt." Coop glanced at his daughter in the rearview mirror and an overwhelming urge to climb into the backseat and give her a big hug overcame him. God, he'd been so close to losing her.

When he'd left Kendall's, he'd decided to pick up Steffi from the Fletchers' house early instead of heading right back to work. She was practically jumping in her seat at the prospect of having Kendall over for dinner. Kendall had made quite an impression on his daughter.

Raindrops began to pelt his windshield, and he gave Steffi a reassuring smile. "There won't be much rain in Arizona, at least not like this—cold and gray."

"Good." She had her forehead pressed against the window and was breathing onto the glass to create a misty patch. She started wiggling her finger through the condensation. "Daddy?"

"What, Tiger Lily." Steffi had recently become a big fan of Peter Pan.

"Who's Stevie?"

"Stevie?" He made the next turn, pumping his

brakes. "I don't know a Stevie. Is that someone new in class?"

"No, the man said Stevie."

His pulse sped up. "What man?"

"You know. The man."

"The man who took you?"

"Uh-huh."

"I thought you said you didn't hear him speak. He didn't talk to you."

"Not really to me. It was when I was falling asleep, after he put the stuff on my mouth."

"What did he say, Steffi? What did he say about Stevie?" His heart banged against his rib cage, and he had to pull the truck over.

"He said like in a whisper, 'It was always you, Stevie. Everything was about Stevie.'" She rubbed her fist across the window. "Who's Stevie?"

Coop swallowed hard. Stevie Carson, Wyatt's brother, kidnapped with Kendall's sister and the other little girl, Heather Brice.

Wyatt, afraid of Buddy. Wyatt, a hunter. Wyatt, the hero who knew just where to find the kids. Wyatt, alone with Kendall at her house.

Cranking the wheel, he made a U-turn in the middle of the street. "I forgot something at work, Steffi. Do you mind hanging out with Genevieve for a little while longer before dinner?"

"No, but who's Stevie? You never said who Stevie was."

"He was a little boy, Steffi. A little boy who lived here a long time ago."

"Did he hate the rain, too?"

"Yeah, I think he did."

Coop dropped Steffi back at the Fletchers', trying to keep a poker face. The anxious looks in their eyes told him he'd failed.

He raced back to Kendall's house but parked his truck down the block. His chest almost exploded with relief when he spied Wyatt's plumbing truck and Aunt Cass's old jalopy in the driveway.

Maybe he was way off base here. Maybe Steffi was mistaken, or maybe the kidnapper, Binder, was obsessed with the Timberline Trio. He didn't know, but he couldn't take any chances.

He'd missed all the warning signs of his wife's condition and he had no intention of ignoring his gut now.

He crept around the side of the house where Buddy's yelps assaulted his ears. As he stepped around the back, he spotted the dog practically doing flips in the pen.

Buddy stopped barking when he noticed Coop, and he mumbled a curse under his breath. Would Buddy's silence draw Wyatt's attention?

Coop sidled along the wall of the house to the back door, cardboard covering the window he'd broken two days ago to get into Kendall's house.

Voices wafted from the dining area off the kitchen, and Coop peeled back a corner of the cardboard.

Hot rage blinded his vision for a split second when he got a look at Kendall bound to a kitchen chair with the silver electrical tape she'd been using to pack up boxes. Wyatt stood in front of her wielding a knife, talking.

Coop withdrew his .45 and took aim.

Wyatt moved out of range, but Coop could still hear his voice.

"You remember how it was, don't you, Kendall? Kayla and Stevie, Kayla and Stevie, oh, and Heather. That's all we heard about. Their pictures were in the paper. People tied ribbons on trees for them. My parents looked at me like they wished I had been kidnapped instead of Stevie." He stepped into view again for a moment as he shook the knife in Kendall's face. "Don't tell me your parents didn't do the same. I mean, your mom even went nuts."

"They were kidnapped, Wyatt. You almost sound jealous."

"I was…for a while, and then we got some attention, didn't we? The siblings that were left behind. So it got better."

"Got better? It never got better."

"For a while it did, and then all the excitement died down. They were never found and Heather's family moved away and you became the popular girl in school and I became nothing."

"You're not nothing, Wyatt. Y-you're a good man."

He laughed and the edge of madness in the sound made Coop clench his teeth.

"I wasn't really, Kendall. I pretended. I played the game." He lunged at her and drew back again. "I killed those animals, you know. I don't hate animals, except Buddy, but I do like to watch them die. Hunting's not good enough for that."

"So, why did you do it? Why'd you kidnap Harrison and Cheri and Steffi?"

"To create another Timberline Trio. I was interviewed when Harrison went missing. Did you see me on TV?"

"I missed that."

C'mon, you son of a bitch. Give me one shot.

"It was good. I didn't want to kill the kids, though, not really. It was different from killing an animal. So then I got a better idea. I'd kidnap one more and then rush in and save them all. And it worked, too."

"I don't think it would've worked in the end, Wyatt. The case against Gary is already starting to fall apart."

Wyatt swore. "That druggie ex-con."

"Why'd you drag me into it? Why the ribbon, the mannequin, the photos buried on my property?"

Wyatt came close to Kendall's chair again and Coop raised his weapon. Then, like prey sensing a predator, Wyatt shuffled back again.

"It made the story more exciting. I was doing you a favor, Kendall. Everyone in town was talking about you. It even got you hooked up with the sheriff." He laughed. "You should be thanking me."

"But you shot at me. You tried to kill me in Port Angeles. Are you going to tell me that wasn't you?"

"Guilty. That wasn't part of my original plan, but I went to see that woman you recommended, Dr. Shipman. I don't know. She put a spell on me or something. I started telling her about how Stevie's kidnapping made me feel. I told her about the animals. When you went out to see her that day, I thought she was going to tell you everything."

"She wouldn't. Everything is confidential."

"I read all about therapy. It's not confidential when someone's committed a crime."

"Did you tell her you kidnapped those children?"

"No, but I could tell by her face she knew something." Wyatt tapped on the wall. "Just like I could tell by your face that you knew once you saw that damned check. Who knew you spelled your name with two *l*'s?"

"And Chuck Rawlings? What happened to him?"

"That was just an accident. He saw me with the pink ribbon, and then I noticed him following you that night in town. I was afraid he was going to talk to you then, so I faked that panic attack for you. Dumbest move ever...except for writing that check."

"You never got a dinosaur."

"Nope, but I had to make sure Rawlings didn't talk to you. I knew he wouldn't go to your house to see you. Creepy perv."

Takes one to know one. Coop tightened his finger on the trigger.

"So, I went to his house, and we had an argument. I might've grabbed him, and then he pulled away and fell. I got the hell out of there, but that stupid dog knew me. I should've taken him out before I left."

"Wyatt, just stop now. You're not going to get away with any of this, and if Rawlings's death was an accident, you haven't killed anyone. You didn't harm the kids. I could testify on your behalf. We could get you some help. Y-you'd even get a lot of attention and publicity."

Coop nodded. Smart girl.

"You didn't mean to kill Gary, did you? You were just thinking of framing him for the kidnappings."

"Naw, the little bit of poison I slipped into his sandwich when he left for the hardware store did just what it was supposed to do—make him sick and make him take off—in case someone wanted to pin the Port Angeles shooting on him. Not that the guy could hit a barn door with a water hose."

"How'd you get to Port Angeles so fast after poisoning Gary's sandwich?"

"The old shortcut, Kendall. It's rough, but it's fast."

"You haven't killed anyone, Wyatt. You can get out of this. It's totally understandable what you did. You're suffering from post-traumatic stress disorder due to Stevie's kidnapping. I can help you."

"It's too late Kendall with two *l*'s. Now that I'm a hero, that's even better than regular attention. I'm a hero. The town's gonna throw me a parade."

"You won't get away with it, Wyatt."

"I think I will, but there's one problem."

"What's that?"

"Like you said, I haven't killed anyone yet and it's too hard doing it up close like this."

"Because you're not a killer. Let's stop this right now."

"Sorry, Kendall. We're just gonna do this a little differently. You see, I can hunt just fine. I can kill when my human target isn't right under my nose—and that's how I'm gonna kill you. I'm gonna hunt you on Aunt Cass's property."

Kendall gasped and choked. "Stop, Wyatt. You can't do this."

"Sure, I can. I have my hunting rifle in my truck. Same one I used on you in Port Angeles. I would've had you that day except for Coop."

"He'll never let you get away with this. It's broad daylight. Your truck's parked in front of my house."

"There's nobody around. I'll make it work. I can even destroy that security setup you have."

Finally, he moved into Coop's range. As Wyatt leaned forward to secure the tape binding Kendall, Coop took his shot.

Kendall screamed and Wyatt clutched his side, spinning around.

Coop ripped the rest of the cardboard from the window and took aim again. "Drop the knife, Wyatt."

Instead of taking his advice, Wyatt raised his knife and turned toward Kendall.

Coop shot him in the chest and Wyatt dropped to the floor, his knife clattering on the linoleum.

Kendall raised shocked eyes to his, and he reached through the door and unlocked it. He was at her side in seconds, wrapping her in his arms as he used his own knife to slice through the electrical tape.

When he freed her, she jumped from the chair, knocking it over, and launched herself at his chest. She sobbed against his shoulder. "I knew you'd come back."

Stroking her hair, he kissed her tears that fell like raindrops on her face.

She glanced down at Wyatt's still form. "I guess he'll get what he always wanted—fame."

Coop corrected her. "Infamy."

Epilogue

Holding a glass of lemonade in each hand, Kendall nudged open the screen door with her hip and her flip-flops smacked against the patio. She sat on the edge of the chaise lounge where Coop sprawled, one leg hanging off the side.

She set down the glasses and rubbed one hand across his warm chest. "You're going to be a bronzed god in no time."

"You have cold hands." He captured her wrist and kissed her palm. "But a warm, warm heart."

"Is Gary doing okay?"

"Speaking of your warm heart." He took a sip of lemonade and puckered his lips. "Binder's doing fine. He started a little landscaping business with the truck and tools you gave him."

"Do that thing again with your lips." She puckered her own and he beat her to the kiss.

She took a sip of lemonade to cool down. "The new owners are going to tear down Aunt Cass's house, aren't they?"

"They are." He brushed one knuckle across her cheek. "Are you happy about that?"

"Yes—too much tragedy. Although I should consider myself lucky that I didn't go off the deep end like Wyatt."

"You don't think he was already twisted and his brother's kidnapping was the final straw?"

"I'm not sure, but I don't think he was killing animals before the Timberline Trio kidnappings and, of course, he was too young to have had anything to do with those kidnappings."

He squeezed her knee. "I'm just happy Steffi remembered what Wyatt had said about Stevie."

"I am, too. I helped her and she helped me. I think we have the beginning of a great relationship." She crowded onto the chaise lounge next to him, dropping her head to his shoulder. "Is she excited about moving to Arizona when your new job starts?"

"She's sad about leaving her friends, but she can't wait." He tangled his fingers through her hair. "And neither can I."

"I think we're right to have separate places at first, don't you?" Her tongue darted from her mouth to taste his salty skin.

He growled in her ear. "When you do stuff like that to me, I think it's the dumbest idea on the planet to have separate places, but for Steffi's sake, I think we're doing the right thing. We'll do it right—wedding in a year, a sibling in a year."

She snuggled in closer, hooking her leg around his. "Or two or three."

"Siblings?"

"Years."

"You haven't changed your mind about having kids,

have you?" He tugged a lock of her hair. "I know kids weren't always in your game plan."

"My game plan started to change the day I met you."

After several long kisses, they came up for air and Coop sucked down the rest of his lemonade. "You know, we never got any closer to figuring out what happened to the Timberline Trio."

Kendall squinted at the sun glinting off the water in the pool and stretched her arms toward the warmth. "I'll leave that mystery for someone else to solve. I know in my heart that five-year-old Kendall did everything she could to save her twin. And grownup Kendall has nothing to prove."

"Not so fast, grownup Kendall." Coop trailed a hand down her back. "This is my last night in Phoenix before I go back to cold, rainy Timberline, and you still have a few things to prove to me."

She pushed up from the chaise lounge and grabbed his hands. "Then what are we waiting for?"

* * * * *

*Look for SUDDEN SECOND CHANCE,
the next book in Carol Ericson's
TARGET: TIMBERLINE miniseries.
You'll find it in September wherever
Harlequin Intrigue books are sold!*

THE MONTANA HAMILTONS *Series*
by B.J. Daniels goes on.
Turn the page for a sneak peek at INTO DUST...

CHAPTER ONE

THE CEMETERY SEEMED unusually quiet. Jack Durand paused on the narrow walkway to glance toward the Houston skyline. He never came to Houston without stopping by his mother's grave. He liked to think of his mother here in this beautiful, peaceful place. And he always brought flowers. Today he'd brought her favorite: daisies.

He breathed in the sweet scent of freshly mown lawn as he moved through shafts of sunlight fingering their way down through the huge oak trees. Long shadows fell across the path, offering a breath of cooler air. Fortunately, the summer day wasn't hot and the walk felt good after the long drive in from the ranch.

The silent gravestones and statues gleamed in the sun. His favorites were the angels. He liked the idea of all the angels here watching over his mother, he thought, as he passed the small lake ringed with trees and followed the wide bend of Braes Bayou situated along one side of the property. A flock of ducks took flight, flapping wildly and sending water droplets into the air.

He'd taken the long way because he needed to relax.

He knew it was silly, but he didn't want to visit his mother upset. He'd promised her on her deathbed that he would try harder to get along with his father.

Ahead, he saw movement near his mother's grave and slowed. A man wearing a dark suit stood next to the angel statue that watched over her final resting place. The man wasn't looking at the grave or the angel. Instead, he appeared to simply be waiting impatiently. As he turned…

With a start, Jack recognized his father.

He thought he had to be mistaken at first. Tom Durand had made a point of telling him he would be in Los Angeles the next few days. Had his father's plans changed? Surely he would have no reason to lie about it.

Until recently, that his father might have lied would never have occurred to him. But things had been strained between them since Jack had told him he wouldn't be taking over the family business.

It wasn't just seeing his father here when he should have been in Los Angeles. It was seeing him in this cemetery. He knew for a fact that his father hadn't been here since the funeral.

"I don't like cemeteries," he'd told his son when Jack had asked why he didn't visit his dead wife. "Anyway, what's the point? She's gone."

Jack felt close to his mother near her grave. "It's a sign of respect."

His father had shaken his head, clearly displeased with the conversation. "We all mourn in our own ways. I like to remember your mother my own way, so lay off, okay?"

So why the change of heart? Not that Jack wasn't glad to see it. He knew that his parents had loved each other. Kate Durand had been sweet and loving, the perfect match for Tom, who was a distant workaholic.

Jack was debating joining him or leaving him to have this time alone with his wife, when he saw another man approaching his father. He quickly stepped behind a monument. Jack was far enough away that he didn't recognize the man right away. But while he couldn't see the man's face clearly from this distance, he recognized the man's limp.

Jack had seen him coming out of the family import/export business office one night after hours. He'd asked his father about him and been told Ed Urdahl worked on the docks.

Now he frowned as he considered why either of the men was here. His father hadn't looked at his wife's grave even once. Instead he seemed to be in the middle of an intense conversation with Ed. The conversation ended abruptly when his father reached into his jacket pocket and pulled out a thick envelope and handed it to the man.

He watched in astonishment as Ed pulled a wad of money from the envelope and proceeded to count it. Even from where he stood, Jack could tell that the gesture irritated his father. Tom Durand expected everyone to take what he said or did as the gospel.

Ed finished counting the money, put it back in the envelope and stuffed it into his jacket pocket. His father seemed to be giving Ed orders. Then looking around as if worried they might have been seen, Tom Durand turned and walked away toward an exit on the other side of the cemetery—the one farthest from the reception building. He didn't even give a backward glance to his wife's grave. Nor had he left any flowers for her. Clearly, his reason for being here had nothing to do with Kate Durand.

Jack was too stunned to move for a moment. What had that exchange been about? Nothing legal, he thought. A hard knot formed in his stomach. What was his father involved in?

He noticed that Ed was heading in an entirely different direction. Impulsively, he began to follow him, worrying about what his father had paid the man to do.

Ed headed for a dark green car parked in the lot near where Jack himself had parked earlier. Jack dropped the daisies, exited the cemetery yards behind him and headed to his ranch pickup. Once behind the wheel, he followed as Ed left the cemetery.

Staying a few cars back, he tailed the man, all the time trying to convince himself that there was a rational explanation for the strange meeting in the cemetery or his father giving this man so much money. But it just didn't wash. His father hadn't been there to visit his dead wife. So what was Tom Durand up to?

Jack realized that Ed was headed for an older part of Houston that had been gentrified in recent years. A row of brownstones ran along a street shaded in trees. Small cafés and quaint shops were interspersed with the brownstones. Because it was late afternoon, the street wasn't busy.

Ed pulled over, parked and cut his engine. Jack turned into a space a few cars back, noticing that Ed still hadn't gotten out.

Had he spotted the tail? Jack waited, half expecting Ed to emerge and come stalking toward his truck. And what? Beat him up? Call his father?

So far all Ed had done from what Jack could tell was sit and watch a brownstone across the street.

Jack continued to observe the green car, wondering how long he was going to sit here waiting for something to happen. This was crazy. He had no idea what had transpired at the cemetery. While the transaction had looked suspicious, maybe his father had really been visiting his mother's grave and told Ed to meet him there so he could pay him money he owed him. But for what that required such a large amount of cash? And why in the cemetery?

Even as Jack thought it, he still didn't believe what he'd seen was innocent. He couldn't shake the feeling that his father had hired the man for some kind of job that involved whoever lived in that brownstone across the street.

He glanced at the time. Earlier, when he'd decided to stop by the cemetery, he knew he'd be cutting it close to meet his appointment back at the ranch. He prided himself on his punctuality. But if he kept sitting here, he would miss his meeting.

Jack reached for his cell phone. The least he could do was call and reschedule. But before he could key in the number, the door of the brownstone opened and a young woman with long blond hair came out.

As she started down the street in the opposite direction, Ed got out of his car. Jack watched him make a quick call on his cell phone as he began to follow the woman.

CHAPTER TWO

THE BLONDE HAD the look of a rich girl, from her long coiffed hair to her stylish short skirt and crisp white top to the pale blue sweater lazily draped over one arm. Hypnotized by the sexy swish of her skirt, Jack couldn't miss the glint of silver jewelry at her slim wrist or the name-brand bag she carried.

Jack grabbed the gun he kept in his glove box and climbed out of his truck. The blonde took a quick call on her cell phone as she walked. She quickened her steps, pocketing her phone. Was she meeting someone and running late? A date?

As she turned down another narrow street, he saw Ed on the opposite side of the street on his phone again. Telling someone…what?

He felt his anxiety rise as Ed ended his call and put away his phone as he crossed the street. Jack took off after the two. He tucked the gun into the waist of his jeans. He had no idea what was going on, but all his instincts told him the blonde, whoever she was, was in danger.

As he reached the corner, he saw that Ed was now only yards behind the woman, his limp even more pro-

nounced. The narrow alley-like street was empty of
people and businesses. The neighborhood rejuvenation
hadn't reached this street yet. There was dirt and debris along the front of the vacant buildings. So where
was the woman going?

Jack could hear the blonde's heels making a *tap, tap,
tap* sound as she hurried along. Ed's work boots made
no sound as he gained on the woman.

As Ed increased his steps, he pulled out what looked
like a white cloth from a plastic bag in his pocket. Discarding the bag, he suddenly rushed down the deserted
street toward the woman.

Jack raced after him. Ed had reached the woman,
looping one big strong arm around her from behind
and lifting her off her feet. Her blue sweater fell to the
ground along with her purse as she struggled.

Ed was fighting to get the cloth over her mouth and
nose. The blonde was frantically moving her head back
and forth and kicking her legs and arms wildly. Some
of her kicks were connecting. Ed let out several cries
of pain as well as a litany of curses as she managed to
knock the cloth from his hand.

After setting her feet on the ground, Ed grabbed a
handful of her hair and jerked her head back. Cocking
his other fist, he reared back as if to slug her.

Running up, Jack pulled the gun, and hit the man
with the stock of his handgun.

Ed released his hold on the woman's hair, stumbled
and fell to his knees as she staggered back from him,
clearly shaken. Her gaze met his as Jack heard a vehicle roaring toward them from another street. Unless
he missed his guess, it was cohorts of Ed's.

As a van came careening around the corner, Jack cried "Come on!" to the blonde. She stood a few feet away looking too stunned and confused to move. He quickly stepped to her, grabbed her hand and, giving her only enough time to pick up her purse from the ground, pulled her down the narrow alley.

Behind them, the van came to a screeching stop. Jack looked back to see two men in the front of the vehicle. One jumped out to help Ed, who was holding the blonde's sweater to his bleeding head.

Jack tugged on her arm and she began to run with him again. They rounded a corner, then another one. He thought he heard the sound of the van's engine a block over and wanted to keep running, but he could tell she wasn't up to it. He dragged her into an inset open doorway to let her catch her breath.

They were both breathing hard. He could see that she was still scared, but the shock seemed to be wearing off. She eyed him as if having second thoughts about letting a complete stranger lead her down this dark alley.

"I'm not going to hurt you," he said. "I'm trying to protect you from those men who tried to abduct you."

She nodded, but didn't look entirely convinced. "Who are you?"

"Jack. My name is Jack Durand. I saw that man following you," he said. "I didn't think, I just ran up behind him and hit him." It was close enough to the truth. "Who are *you*?"

"Cassidy Hamilton." No Texas accent. Nor did the name ring any bells. So what had they wanted with this young woman?

"Any idea who those guys were or why they were after you?"

She looked away, swallowed, then shook her head. "Do you think they're gone?"

"I don't think so." After he'd seen that wad of money his father had given Ed, he didn't think the men would be giving up. "I suspect they are now looking for both of us." When he'd looked back earlier, he'd thought Ed or one of the other men had seen him. He'd spent enough time at his father's warehouse that most of the dockworkers knew who he was.

But why would his father want this woman abducted? It made no sense and yet it was the only logical conclusion he could draw given what he'd witnessed at the cemetery.

"Let's wait a little bit. Do you live around here?"

"I was staying with a friend."

"I don't think you should go back there. That man has been following you for several blocks."

She nodded and hugged herself, looking scared. He figured a lot of what had almost happened hadn't yet registered. Either that or what had almost happened didn't come as a complete surprise to her. Which made him even more curious why his father would want to abduct this woman.

ED URDAHL COULDN'T believe his luck. He'd picked a street that he knew wouldn't have anyone on it this time of the day. On top of that, the girl had been in her own little world. She hadn't been paying any attention to him as he'd moved up directly behind her.

The plan had been simple. Grab her, toss her into

the van that would come speeding up at the perfect time and make a clean, quick getaway so no one would be the wiser.

It should have gone down without any trouble.

He'd been so intent on the woman in front of him, though, that he hadn't heard the man come up behind him until it was too late. Even if someone had intervened, Ed had been pretty sure he could handle it. He'd been a wrestler and boxer growing up. Few men were stupid enough to take him on.

The last thing he'd expected was to be smacked in the back of the head by some do-gooder. What had he been hit with anyway? Something hard and cold. A gun? The blow had knocked him senseless and the next thing he'd known he was on the sidewalk bleeding. As he'd heard the van engine roaring in his direction, he'd fought to keep from blacking out as whoever had blindsided him had gotten away with the blonde.

"What happened?" his brother Alec demanded now. Ed leaned against the van wall in the back, his head hurting like hell. "I thought you had it all worked out."

"How the hell do I know?" He was still bleeding like a stuck pig. "Just get out of here. *Drive!*" he yelled at the driver, Nick, a dockworker he'd used before for less-than-legal jobs. "Circle the block until I can think of what to do."

Ed caught a whiff of the blonde's perfume and realized he was holding her sweater to his bleeding skull. He took another sniff of it. *Nice.* He tried to remember exactly what had transpired. It had all happened so fast. "Did you see who hit me?" he asked.

"I saw a man and a woman going down the alley," Alec said. "I thought you said she'd be alone?"

That's what he had thought. It had all been set up in a way that should have gone off like clockwork. So where had whoever hit him come from? "So neither of you got a look at the guy?"

Nick cleared his throat. "I thought at first that he was working *with* you."

"Why would you think that?" Ed demanded, his head hurting too much to put up with such stupid remarks. "The son of a bitch coldcocked me with something."

"A gun. It was a gun," Alec said. "I saw the light catch on the metal when he tucked it back into his pants."

"He was carrying a gun?" Ed sat up, his gaze going to Nick. "Is that why you thought he was part of the plan?"

"No, I didn't see the gun," Nick said. "I just assumed he was in on it because of who he was."

Ed pressed the sweet-smelling sweater to his head and tried not to erupt. "Are you going to make me guess? Or are you frigging going to tell me who was he?"

"Jack Durand."

"What?" Ed couldn't believe his ears. What were the chances that Tom Durand's son would show up on this particular street? Unless his father had sent him? That made no sense. *Why pay me if he sent his son?*

"You're sure it was Jack?"

"Swear on my mother's grave," Nick said as he drove in wider circles. "I saw him clear as a bell. He turned in the alley to look back. It was Jack, all right."

"Go back to that alley," Ed ordered. Was this Tom's backup plan in case Ed failed? Or was this all part of Tom's real plan? Either way, it appeared Jack Durand had the girl.

CASSIDY LOOKED AS if she might make a run for it at any moment. That would be a huge mistake on her part. But Jack could tell that she was now pretty sure she shouldn't be trusting him. He wasn't sure how much longer he could keep her here. She reached for her phone, but he laid a hand on her arm.

"That's the van coming back," he said quietly. At the sound of the engine growing nearer, he signaled her not to make a sound as he pulled her deeper into the darkness of the doorway recess. The van drove slowly up the alley. He'd feared they would come back. That's why he'd been hesitant to move from their hiding place.

Jack held his breath as he watched the blonde, afraid she might do something crazy like decide to take her chances and run. He wouldn't have blamed her. For all she knew, he could have been in on the abduction and was holding her here until the men in the van came back for her.

The driver of the van braked next to the open doorway. The engine sat idling. Jack waited for the sound of a door opening. He'd put the gun into the back waistband of his jeans before he'd grabbed the blonde, thinking the gun might frighten her. As much as he wanted to pull it now, he talked himself out of it.

At least for the moment. He didn't want to get involved in any gunplay—especially with the young woman here. He'd started carrying the gun when he'd worked for his father and had to take the day's proceeds to a bank drop late at night. It was a habit he'd gotten used to even after he'd quit. Probably because of the type of people who worked with his father.

After what seemed like an interminable length of time, the van driver pulled away.

Jack let out the breath he'd been holding. "Come on. I'll see that you get someplace safe where you can call the police," he said and held out his hand.

She hesitated before she took it. They moved through the dark shadows of the alley to the next street. The sky above them had turned a deep silver in the evening light. It was still hot, little air in the tight, narrow street.

He realized that wherever Cassidy Hamilton had been headed, she hadn't planned to return until much later—thus the sweater. He wanted to question her, but now wasn't the time.

At the edge of the buildings, Jack peered down the street. He didn't see the van or Ed's green car. But he also didn't think they had gone far. Wouldn't they expect her to call the police? The area would soon be crawling with cop cars. So what would Ed do?

A few blocks from the deserted area where they'd met, they reached a more commercial section. The street was growing busier as people got off work. Restaurants began opening for the evening meal as boutiques and shops closed. Jack spotted a small bar with just enough patrons that he thought they could blend in.

"Let's go in here," he said. "I don't know about you, but I could use a drink. You should be able to make a call from here. Once I know you're safe…"

They took a table at the back away from the television over the bar. He removed his Stetson and put it on the seat next to him. When Cassidy wasn't looking, he removed the .45 from the waistband of his jeans and slid it under the hat.

"What do you want to drink?" he asked as the waitress approached.

"White wine," she said and plucked nervously at the torn corner of her blouse. Other than the torn blouse, she looked fine physically. But emotionally, he wasn't sure how much of a toll this would take on her over the long haul. That was if Ed didn't find her.

"I'll have whiskey," he said, waving the waitress off. He had no idea what he was going to do now. He told himself he just needed a jolt of alcohol. He'd been playing this by ear since seeing his father and Ed at the cemetery.

Now he debated what he was going to do with this woman given the little he knew. The last thing he wanted, though, was to get involved with the police. He was sure Ed and his men had seen him, probably recognized him. Once his father found out that it had been his son who'd saved the blonde...

The waitress put two drinks in front of them and left. He watched the blonde take a sip. She'd said her name was Cassidy Hamilton. She'd also said she didn't know why anyone would want to abduct her off the street, but he suspected that wasn't true.

"So is your old man rich or something?" he asked and took a gulp of the whiskey.

She took a sip of her wine as if stalling, her gaze lowered. He got his first really good look at her. She was a knockout. When she lifted her eyes finally, he thought he might drown in all that blue.

"I only ask because I'm trying to understand why those men were after you." She could be a famous model or even an actress. He didn't follow pop culture, hardly ever watched television and hadn't been to the movies in ages. All he knew was, at the very least, she'd grown up with money. "If you're famous or something, I apologize for not knowing."

REQUEST YOUR FREE BOOKS!
2 FREE NOVELS PLUS 2 FREE GIFTS!

H HARLEQUIN®

INTRIGUE

BREATHTAKING ROMANTIC SUSPENSE

YES! Please send me 2 FREE Harlequin® Intrigue novels and my 2 FREE gifts (gifts are worth about $10). After receiving them, if I don't wish to receive any more books, I can return the shipping statement marked "cancel." If I don't cancel, I will receive 6 brand-new novels every month and be billed just $4.74 per book in the U.S. or $5.49 per book in Canada. That's a savings of at least 12% off the cover price! It's quite a bargain! Shipping and handling is just 50¢ per book in the U.S. and 75¢ per book in Canada.* I understand that accepting the 2 free books and gifts places me under no obligation to buy anything. I can always return a shipment and cancel at any time. Even if I never buy another book, the two free books and gifts are mine to keep forever.

182/382 HDN GH3D

Name   (PLEASE PRINT)

Address   Apt. #

City   State/Prov.   Zip/Postal Code

Signature (if under 18, a parent or guardian must sign)

Mail to the **Reader Service:**
IN U.S.A.: P.O. Box 1867, Buffalo, NY 14240-1867
IN CANADA: P.O. Box 609, Fort Erie, Ontario L2A 5X3
**Are you a subscriber to Harlequin® Intrigue books
and want to receive the larger-print edition?
Call 1-800-873-8635 or visit www.ReaderService.com.**

* Terms and prices subject to change without notice. Prices do not include applicable taxes. Sales tax applicable in N.Y. Canadian residents will be charged applicable taxes. Offer not valid in Quebec. This offer is limited to one order per household. Not valid for current subscribers to Harlequin Intrigue books. All orders subject to credit approval. Credit or debit balances in a customer's account(s) may be offset by any other outstanding balance owed by or to the customer. Please allow 4 to 6 weeks for delivery. Offer available while quantities last.

Your Privacy—The Reader Service is committed to protecting your privacy. Our Privacy Policy is available online at www.ReaderService.com or upon request from the Reader Service.

We make a portion of our mailing list available to reputable third parties that offer products we believe may interest you. If you prefer that we not exchange your name with third parties, or if you wish to clarify or modify your communication preferences, please visit us at www.ReaderService.com/consumerschoice or write to us at Reader Service Preference Service, P.O. Box 9062, Buffalo, NY 14240-9062. Include your complete name and address.

Natalie's car suddenly swerved. Tension snapped through
Clint. She barreled off the road and into the lot of a
supermarket, crashing broadside into a parked car.

His pulse hammering, Clint made the turn and skidded
to a stop next to her car. He jumped out and rushed to her.
Thank God no one was in the other vehicle. Natalie sat
upright behind the steering wheel. The deflated air bag
sagged in front of her. The injuries she may have sustained
from the air bag deploying ticked off in his brain.

He tried to open the door but it was locked. He banged
on the window. "Natalie! Are you all right?"

She turned and stared up at him. Her face was flushed
red, abrasions already darkening on her skin. His heart
rammed mercilessly against his sternum as she slowly hit
the unlock button. He yanked the door open and crouched
down to get a closer look at her.

"Are you hurt?" he demanded.

"I'm not sure." She took a deep breath as if she'd only just remembered to breathe. "I don't understand what happened. I was driving along and the air bag suddenly burst from the steering wheel." She reached for the wheel and then drew back, uncertain what to do with her hands. "I don't understand," she repeated.

"I'm calling for help." Clint made the call to 9-1-1 and then he called his friend Lieutenant Chet Harper. Every instinct cautioned Clint that Natalie was wrong about not being able to trust herself.

There was someone else—someone very close to her—she shouldn't trust. He intended to keep her safe until he identified that threat.

Don't miss DARK WHISPERS
by USA TODAY *bestselling author Debra Webb,*
available in September 2016 wherever
Harlequin® Intrigue books and ebooks are sold.

www.Harlequin.com

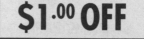

$1.⁰⁰ OFF

$7.99 U.S./$9.99 CAN.

New York Times Bestselling Author

B.J. DANIELS

He's meant to protect her, but what is this cowboy keeping from her about the danger she's facing?

INTO DUST

Available July 26, 2016.
Pick up your copy today!

HQN™

$1.⁰⁰ OFF

the purchase price of INTO DUST by B.J. Daniels.

Offer valid from July 26, 2016 to August 31, 2016.
Redeemable at participating retail outlets. Not redeemable at Barnes & Noble.
Limit one coupon per purchase. Valid in the U.S.A. and Canada only.

52613799

5 65373 00076 2   (8100)0 12169

JUST CAN'T GET ENOUGH?

Join our social communities
and talk to us online.

You will have access to the latest
news on upcoming titles and special
promotions, but most importantly,
you can talk to other fans about your
favorite Harlequin reads.

Harlequin.com/Community